MIND YOUR BRAIN
MASTER YOUR LIFE

Also by Sirshree

Spiritual Masterpieces- Self Realisation books for serious seekers

Who Am I Now: From mindfulness to no-mind
Answers that Awaken: Access the Source of Wisdom within You
100% Karma: Learn the Art of Concious Karma that Liberates
100% Wisdom: Wisdom that leads you to experience and be established in your true nature
100% Meditation: Dip into the Stillness of Pure Awareness
You are Meditation : Discover Peace and Bliss Within
Essence of Devotion: From Devotee to Divinity
The Unshaken Mind: Discovering the Purpose, Power and Potential of your mind
The Supreme Quest: Your search for the Truth ends there where you are
The Greatest Freedom: Discover the key to an Awakened Living

Self Help Treasures - Self Development books for success seekers

The Source of Health: The Key to Perfect Health Discovery
Inner Ninety Hidden Infinity: How to build your book of values
Inner 90 for Youth: The secret of reaching and staying at the peak of success
The Source for Youth: You have the power to change your life
Inner Magic: The Power of self-talk
Self Encounter: The Complete Path - Self Development to Self Realization
The Five Supreme Secrets of Life: Unveiling the Ways to Attain Wealth, Love and God
You are Not Lazy: A story of shifting from Laziness to Success
Freedom From Fear, Worry, Anger: How to be cool, calm and courageous

New Age Nuggets - Practical books on applied spirituality and self help

The Source: Power of Happy Thoughts
Secret of Happiness: Instant Happiness - Here and Now!
Excuse me God...: Fulfilling your wishes through the Power of Prayer and Seed of Faith
Help God to Help You: Whatever you do, do it with a smile
Ultimate Purpose of Success: Achieving Success in all five aspects of life
Celebrating Relationships: Bringing Love, Life, Laughter in Your Relations
Everything is a Game of Beliefs: Understanding is the Whole Thing

Profound Parables - Fiction books containing profound truths

Beyond Life: Conversations on Life After Death
The One Above: What if God was your neighbour?
The Warrior's Mirror: The Path To Peace
Master of Siddhartha: Revealing the Truth of Life and After-life
Put Stress to Rest: Utilizing Stress to Make Progress
The Source @ Work: A Story of Inspiration from Jeeodee

MIND YOUR BRAIN MASTER YOUR LIFE

PRACTICAL METHODS TO CREATE
HEALTHY PATHWAYS IN YOUR BRAIN

A Happy Thoughts Initiative

Mind Your Brain, Master Your Life
Practical Methods to Create Healthy Pathways in Your Brain
By Tejgyan Global Foundation

Copyright © Tejgyan Global Foundation
All Rights Reserved 2017

Tejgyan Global Foundation is a charitable organization
with its headquarters in Pune, India.

Published by WOW Publishings Pvt. Ltd., India

First edition published in November 2017

_____

Copyrights are reserved with Tejgyan Global Foundation and publishing rights are vested exclusively with WOW Publishings Pvt. Ltd. This book is sold subject to the condition that it shall not by way of trade or otherwise, be lent, resold, hired out, or otherwise circulated without the publisher's prior written consent in any form of binding or cover other than that in which it is published and without a similar condition including this condition being imposed on the subsequent purchaser and without limiting the rights under copyright reserved above, no part of this publication may be reproduced, stored in or introduced into a retrieval system, or transmitted, in any form, or by any means, electronic, mechanical, photocopying, recording or otherwise, without the prior written permission of both the copyright owner and the above-mentioned publisher of this book. Any person who does any unauthorized act in relation to this publication may be liable to criminal prosecution and civil claims for damages.

*To those spiritual masters
who transcended all limitations of the mind
and mastered their life.*

*To those scientists
who unraveled the mysteries of the human brain.*

Contents

Preface ix

1. Why New Year Resolutions Don't Last Long? 1
2. Want to Get Rid of Old Habits? 5
3. Want to Add New Good Habits? 12
4. Want to Overcome Fear? 20
5. The Way to Get What You Want 25
6. How to Handle Uncomfortable Feelings? 29
7. Placebo Effect – Nocebo Effect 39
8. Delayed Gratification 48

9.	Mirror Neurons	55
10.	Be Happy and Attract the Best in Life	63
11.	Symbology	73
12.	Love	84
13.	Freedom from Exaggeration	93
14.	Freedom from Gadgets	101

Preface

Many people feel it's enough to carry on with their same old routine and behavior. They then resolve to start with a new routine on the occasion of a new year. On day one, they are geared up with this intention and start with full force. But with the passage of time, their enthusiasm begins to wane. Gradually, they find themselves falling back to the same old routine. They then wonder what really went wrong. They feel that maybe they lacked in planning and execution and decide to work upon it more vigorously the next year. But the same story repeats every year. They accept that they can't make this radical change in their routine and continue with the way they are.

There are some who want to bring new habits in their daily routine or want to get rid of some of their old habits. For example, although the doctor advises them not to consume sweets, they can't resist temptation. They get overpowered with their uncomfortable feelings and react in the same way they have been used to react to people as well as situations. No matter how hard they try, they can't cope with the change for long. Although they are in search of happiness, at the end they keep switching between happiness and unhappiness.

You will find insights on these and many more topics in the chapters that follow. We have been conditioned with age-old beliefs and die-hard habits since our childhood. Our brains have been ingrained with these habits, resulting in creation of neural pathways. Till now it was believed that our brain can't be changed after a certain age. But with the help of modern science of neuroplasticity, we can learn to rewire our brains. If we want to incorporate new habits, we need to first understand about neural pathways. As we change them in line with our vision, we can bring about a radical transformation in our life. Subsequently, we can attain and sustain our physical fitness, mental stability, financial abundance, harmony in our relationships, and spiritual wellbeing.

This book has 14 chapters covering different topics of neural rewiring. Each chapter delves deeper into a topic with the findings from brain research, its practical application and further insights on it in the light of spiritual understanding.

Though each chapter is complete and independent in itself, while reading for the first time, it is suggested that you read the book from start to finish in order to gain more clarity on the subject. Later, you may directly zoom in on the topic that interests you the most.

Enjoy reading this book and create new neural pathways in order to unleash your highest potential and expression. Best wishes!

1

Why New Year Resolutions Don't Last Long?

The Science of Neural Pathways

Does it happen to you that your new year resolutions seldom last? If yes, then you are not alone. Worldwide statistics shows that more than 90% new year resolutions do not see the light of one full year. One may wonder why is it so?

 Brain Research

Neural pathways of our brain play important role in it. Neurons are nerve cells that transmit nerve signals to and from the brain. The pathway along which information travels through the neurons (nerve cells) of the brain is a neural pathway. As we have been habituated to do things in a certain way, our brain has been ingrained with these neural pathways. In that sense, a lot of the programming of our brain is "hard wired" into it and we also create new neural pathways every time we do or think something new and different. When we make a new year resolution, it is probably a new neural pathway. But the old wiring is so strong that you default back to it.

We can see that innumerable number of neural pathways have been created in our brain since our childhood. These positive and negative pathways were helpful in our childhood for our survival. But as we grow up, some of them are deterrent for our growth. Some of them are quite primitive in nature which doesn't help us sustain in the world we live in. Some of the responses triggered by these neural pathways create conflicts in our lives. So, there is a need to reprogram or rewire these neural pathways in order to help us meet our goals.

 Practical Application

The solution is simple. If you are asked to change your usual route from home to office, what will you do? You will stop taking the usual route and try out new different routes. You will choose the most economical, time-saving one among them and start using it. Will this transition from the old to the new one be quick, smooth and easy? No. Initially you will find yourself on the old route out of habit but soon you will remind yourself of the new route. With consistent practice, you will soon get habituated to the new route.

You need to apply the same principle in case of rewiring the neural pathways. When you take up New Year resolution, you decide to change your neural pathways. It needs perseverance and consistent effort to go through this process of change. But if you fail to do so, you will find yourself on the old neural pathways again.

Thus, the practical application of the research on neural pathways is as follows:

1. Understand the concept of old wiring and that it is difficult to change old wiring.
2. To change new wiring, spend enough time to create new wiring. Start slowly and increase. For example, if you would like to begin exercising, start small.
3. Focus on creating only one new wiring at one time. Don't take on many new habits at the same time.

🪷 Spiritual Insight

We have been conditioned with age-old beliefs, die-hard habits since our childhood out of ignorance. Our parents, neighbors, teachers and media played a key role in doing so. As a child, we saw them glued to the television watching serials or movies. We saw them engrossed in gossip and criticism about food, clothing, entertainment, and people. We saw them enslaved by the latest fashion trends. We saw them ecstatic on receiving sensual pleasures and distressed when they were denied. At that tender age, we lacked the ability to discern. Hence, we just learned and copied what we saw. Not for a moment did we doubt that the programming we'd received could be wrong. We believed it to be our nature to fulfill our cravings. We never considered the source or the basis of our choices in life. Thus, our brains got wired to seek happiness from external objects.

When we receive higher wisdom, we realize the need to identify our past conditioning and get rid of it. We choose to make decisions based on the wisdom we have received and the power of discernment awakened within us. We decide to remain in the state of love, bliss and peace regardless of external circumstances.

We resolve to have physical fitness, stillness of mind, abundance, and harmony in relations. The more spiritual we grow, the more new neural pathways of spiritual habits we would like to build. But our old habits and tendencies don't allow us to follow the new path immediately. We need to consistently walk on the new path until it becomes our nature.

While there are various spiritual pathways, the habits of meditation, spiritual practice (*Sadhana*), chanting, penance, forgiveness and affirmations increase our inner strength and help us in holding back our programmed responses. Understand the concept of neural pathways and slowly and consistently create spiritual habits. The more you listen to discourses, the more you develop faith on the path. The more you contemplate on spiritual wisdom, it becomes easier to create new neural pathways of love, joy and peace.

2

Want to Get Rid of Old Habits?

Habit Replacement

Some children are used to drinking milk. After growing up they feel the need to change this habit but can't give it up. Some grownups find it difficult to give up the habit of biting nails. There are a few who want to get rid of their morning tea or coffee habit, but fail. Most people find it very hard to get rid of their addictions to smoking, junk food, etc. When it comes to bad habits, we manage to do away with the habit for a few days, but later on fall back to the same old routine. Why is it so?

 Brain Research

Let's understand it with the example of drinking your morning cup of tea or coffee. For whatever reason, you may have picked up this habit in your early years. Maybe, you observed others drinking tea or coffee and one day you also tried it out of curiosity. Gradually, it became a habit and you had to have it every day. Now it is so ingrained that if you missed it for a single day, you get a headache.

Initially, your brain didn't have the neural pathway for drinking tea or coffee. As you developed the habit of drinking your morning hot cup of liquid, your brain created the neural pathway in support of that habit. The brain doesn't understand whether the habit is good or bad, it just obeys your behavior. With every repetition of the habit, the neural pathway became stronger and your brain recorded the need to repeat this behavior and got trained to do so. It associated a feeling of pleasure with it. Thereafter, it felt right and safe in reminding you of drinking tea or coffee in the morning. As a result, you developed a craving for it in the morning. After drinking it, you felt pleasure and became energetic. Thus, your brain created a mental fusion of the behavior of drinking tea or coffee, feeling pleasurable and becoming energetic.

Now, if you stop drinking it, it indirectly signals the brain that the mental fusion is at stake. As a result, the brain generates withdrawal symptoms such as headache, restlessness, irritability in an attempt to force you back on the old neural pathway of drinking tea or coffee again.

 Practical Application

Once you identify the existing mental fusion, you need to break it and train the brain to make a new fusion. Justify to your brain how harmful the existing mental fusion is and how healthy the new fusion would be.

For example, if you have several cups of tea or coffee in a day, now train your brain with repeated insights about the harmful effects of having it so much. Tell yourself that you are not in control and this leads to more stress and disappointment in the longer run, not pleasure. Further, it's harmful for your health also and so on. Then reassure your brain about the safety of the new fusion you are going to make.

The new fusion around the feeling of pleasure and becoming energetic could be drinking hot water (maybe with lemon and honey) in the place of tea or coffee in the morning or later in the day. You do this by telling yourself the benefits and more importantly, by carrying out the behavior repeatedly. Tell yourself that drinking hot water in place of tea or coffee flushes all toxins in your body and makes you slim, trim and fit. Whenever there is a craving for tea or coffee, you will drink warm water in order to train your brain to form a new neural pathway. The more you repeat it, the stronger the pathway becomes. As you stop drinking tea or coffee, your old pathway fades away.

Thus, the practical application of the research on neural pathways is as follows:

1. Mental fusion can be created between two things which are not logically or practically linked to each other. They can be behavior, feelings, or thoughts. You can replace the existing habit with a new healthy one. For example, if you want to stop watching TV, go for a walk. If you want to stop smoking, listen to music.

2. Our brain can't discriminate between what we actually see and what we imagine. If we repeatedly visualize the new habit and its positive consequences, our brain assumes it to be the reality and builds the new neural pathway accordingly. The more we repeat it, the stronger the neural pathway becomes and rewires the brain for better results. For example, if you

want to excel in studies, repeatedly visualize yourself studying and scoring well in the exams.

3. Use it or lose it. The neural pathways which are not used for long fade away. The pathways which are traversed often become stronger. Hence, don't focus on the habits you want to get away from. Instead focus on the habits you want to inculcate within and repeat them as often as you can. For example, if you want to practice meditation, do it for a small time but do so every day. With consistent practice, the new pathway will become stronger.

ꙮ Spiritual Insight

As we walk on the path of truth, we wish to inculcate divine qualities like love, joy, peace, harmony, patience, courage, creativity, devotion within us and express them. But during situations, we see that our old tendencies overpower us and we feel negative emotions like anger, boredom, comparison, sorrow, fear, guilt, hatred, ill-will. Sometimes, we even let them out at people. At such times, we may doubt whether we are progressing on the spiritual path.

Suppose you are in a big hall. Now imagine that you have been tied to one end of the hall with a huge rubber band from behind. You are then told that you have to reach the other end of the hall – that's where lies the experience of Self (Consciousness). You have heard that this experience is the most blissful of all experiences and are keen to experience it. You marshal all your strength, move forward against the resistance of the rubber band, and reach that state. You feel so happy that at last you have experienced it. But then you are unable to stay there because the rubber band pulls you back. Each time, reaching and staying in that experience is a struggle.

What does the rubber band signify? It symbolizes your tendencies and habits that pull you back. You are trying to move forward but feeling the pull from behind. You had felt the pull the first time too, but then you had great attraction for the experience. But now the pull of your tendencies comes into play and at the first sign of resistance, you may say, "Ok, I will sit in meditation tomorrow. Looks like I am not in the right mood today. The blissful experience is within me, and I can access it whenever I want." Every time you try to reach the experience, the tendencies pull you back and you drop the idea.

We need to understand that our old habits and tendencies have formed neural pathways in our brain. As we have got habituated to these tendencies since long, the neural pathways have become wider and stronger. Now if we want to replace these old habits with the new habits, it will take time, effort and patience.

For that, a four step process is suggested:

a. Identify the old tendency that is hindering your spiritual growth.

b. Decide a newer and positive mental fusion – a new chain of habit.

c. Tell yourself the negative consequences of the old habit and the benefits of the new spiritual habit.

d. Follow the new habit repeatedly and reaffirm it.

For example, if you become angry at petty issues, remind yourself that you are in favor of the new habit of harboring love, joy and peace. Mentally fuse it with a new behavior of taking a deep breath and feeling peaceful whenever there is a trigger for anger. Tell yourself the consequences of anger you have already been through: the amount of physical and mental suffering you have gone through because of anger, the level of stress built up within you, how anger has spoiled your relationship with people, how it has deteriorated your growth at your workplace. Now, tell yourself the benefits of consciously breathing deeply when you feel angry. Consider how peaceful you would feel, how harmonious your relations could be, how much at ease you would feel; also consider that this can lead to your spiritual growth. Repeatedly carry out this new habit and affirm this to yourself in order to strengthen the new neural pathway.

You can also follow these steps for taking on a new spiritual habit. You need not only use them for getting rid of a bad habit. To grow spiritually, take on habits that enhance the divine qualities of love, joy and peace. When you are listening to discourses, rendering selfless service, immersed in devotion, you are helping in this endeavor. Mentally fuse the habit of volunteering and feeling fulfilled, the habit of writing a journal and feeling gratitude, the habit of praying and feeling blessed. When you repeatedly do any of these activities, you train your brain on new neural pathways and very soon it becomes a part of your regular schedule.

No matter how hard the old neural pathway instigates you to fall back into the old rut, if you are performing spiritual practice (*Sadhana*), you will not fall prey to it. Instead, you will learn to watch your emotions, feelings and thoughts as a witness and respond with equanimity. Every time you practice forgiveness when you hurt someone knowingly or unknowingly by your feelings, thoughts, words or actions, you strengthen a new neural pathway in turn. When you practice chanting, penance, prayer and meditation, you train your brain to make the neural pathways for spiritual growth wider and stronger.

3

Want to Add New Good Habits?

Habit Association

Some people wish to add new good habits. For some days, they manage to work on the new habits using their willpower, but stop in a few days. After many permutations and combinations in their daily routine, they fail to accommodate these new habits. Why is this so? Is there a way around to this?

 Brain Research

Whether we give clear inputs to our brain or not, our brain keeps track of our behavior during the course of a day. It creates a neural pathway for every behavior. Every time we repeat the behavior, the neural pathway becomes stronger. After few repetitions, a time comes when we don't have to consciously repeat the behavior. The brain executes the behavior on its own automatically and the behavior becomes a habit. Thus, whatever activities we repeat from morning till night, our brain creates a neural pathway by linking all the associated neurons together. When we start with the first activity in the morning, the associated neurons fire together to execute the next activities in sequence. The brain has made this automatic, so that we hardly find a scope to change it.

Now, if you want to inculcate some new good habits in your daily routine, you need to associate the new habit with the existing habits. Ensure that you execute these habits at the same time every day. The new neurons related to these habits will get associated with the existing ones in the neural pathway. With repetition, these new neurons will wire and fire together forming a new neural pathway.

 Practical Application

Identify new habits you wish to inculcate in your daily life without disturbing the existing ones. Associate them with your existing habits in such a way that whenever the existing habits trigger, you will execute these new habits. Let's understand it with some examples.

Existing Daily Habits	New Good Habits
Waking up	After waking up, drink a glass of water.
Meals	Before every meal, say a prayer.
Bath	Before having bath, stretch all muscles from head to toe.
Watch TV	Every time when you watch TV, do 2 sit-ups.
Starting your work in office	Before starting your work, take 5 min to plan your work for the day.

Ending your work in office	Just before ending your work, take a 5 min review of your entire day and write down the activities accomplished, activities pending and any showstoppers in completing these activities.
Go to bed at night	Before going to bed, put at least one scattered thing in its appointed place.
Visiting the toilet	Every time you are out of the loo, take 3 deep breaths, stretch out your shoulders and neck, roll them in clockwise and anti-clockwise direction.

Thus, whatever new habits you would like, wire them with existing habits. Do you want to exercise? If you daily drop your son or daughter off to school during weekdays, schedule your exercise routine along with that. At least you will end up exercising during week days. It also helps to make the new habit a small one and gradually increase it. For example, you can decide to walk or run only for five minutes every time you have your morning cup of coffee. Gradually, increase the five minutes to ten to fifteen and so on. You may increase by five minutes every week or even every two weeks. Soon, you will find that it becomes a routine for you to finish your morning cup of coffee and go for a 45-minutes jog.

꧁ Spiritual Insight

To progress on the spiritual path, create new small spiritual habits and associate them with your existing daily habits. Following are some suggested spiritual habits that you can begin small and gradually increase if you would like:

Existing daily habits	New small-spiritual habits
Waking up	Immediately on waking up, you may practice meditation for 17 minutes in 2017. With every year, you can increase this duration by one minute. In 2018, you may meditate for 18 minutes and so on. If you would like, you can begin with five minutes of meditation and increase it.
Brushing your teeth	While brushing your teeth, you may repeat spiritual affirmations such as "My nature is love, joy and peace. I am always happy and at ease."
Bath	While taking bath, you may chant some mantra instead of thinking about anything else. After taking bath, you may say a small prayer.
Meals	Before having meals, you may practice being in gratitude. Thank the farmer who sowed the seeds, the people who brought it from farm to market, the person who brought the grocery to your house and the people who cooked food for you. You may also thank your body which will eat the food and become

	healthy in order to experience and express the qualities of the Self.
Travel	You may listen to spiritual discourses, self-help audios, devotional songs (*bhajans*) on your commute to work.
Starting your work in the office	Take on an intention that God's desire be fulfilled through your body-mind.
During work	Every time you sit down at your desk, take a moment to remember your true nature. Ask yourself, "Who am I?" for a minute.
Ending your work in the office	You may thank God for giving the opportunity to express His divine qualities through your body-mind.
After dinner	Every time you finish having dinner, you can write a journal (a spiritual diary) with your day's lessons.
Going to bed	Before going to bed, you may pr.actice forgiveness with all the people whom you knowingly or unknowingly hurt by your feelings, thoughts, words or actions throughout the day. You may also say goodnight to the space inside you – your true home.

Additionally, you can practice self-centering at specific and unique time of the day. This habit is small, yet powerful one that grounds you throughout the day. The self-centering practice that takes only a couple of minutes every hour has the following three steps:

1. Timing: It is important to decide a unique time every hour. If you are asked to do it every hour, you may agree to do it, but you may not actually do it. So, a unique time-set is recommended. This time is where the hour and minute are same. Thus the recommended time slots throughout the day are as follows: 06:06 a.m., 07:07 a.m., 08:08 a.m. ..... 12:12 p.m., 01:01 p.m., 02:02 p.m. ..... 11:11 p.m., 12:12 a.m., 01:01 a.m. ..... 05:05 a.m.

    If you wake up at 6 in the morning, then you will start at 6:06 and if you retire to bed around 10 in the night, then 10:10 will be your last time slot for practicing self-centering for the day. You need not wake up in the middle of the night at 12:12 or at 1:01.

    Throughout the day, you can arrange for reminders on your computer or set reminders on your cell phone. Thus, you are self-centering every 61st minute except when the transition is from 12:12 to 01:01.

2. Shifting: In this step, use any meditation technique you are aware of to shift to a no-mind state. If you are not aware of any such meditation techniques, you may use any of the techniques viz. watching your breathing, watching your thoughts, or do reverse counting of numbers from 100 to 1. Close your eyes and shift to the heart and remain there at least for a minute.

This step helps you to attune to the stillness within you. By doing that, you allow the Consciousness to experience itself using your body-mind during this period. This tuning also helps you to get in harmony with the nature. As a result, you freely flow with the nature. All the divine qualities like happiness, courage, positivity, creativity, patience shall manifest in your life just by practicing this step every hour.

3. Enquiring: In this step, you become aware of your actions in the past one hour and how you intend your actions in the next one hour. This step reminds you to always operate from your happy natural state.

First enquire about the one hour that passed. Ask yourself the following questions:

- How did I live in the past one hour: Was I in my head or in my heart?
- How many times did I dive into the heart?
- In which incidents did I shift from head to heart or heart to head?

Now, intend to spend the next one hour being more grounded on the heart to operate from a peaceful happy natural state. Ask yourself the following questions:

- How do I intend to live in the next one hour: How will I be established in the heart?
- What all is going to happen in the next one hour: In all incidents, how will I continue to be peaceful and operate from a happy natural state?

Thus, step 1 is about remembering, step 2 is about tuning and step 3 is about awareness. Step 3 helps you to analyze and learn from the past and ensures that you create a beautiful future.

Let us suppose you practiced self-centering at 01:01 p.m. and then could not practice it at 02:02 p.m. and then again remembered at 03:03 p.m. Then, at 03:03 p.m. look at the past 2 hours and the next one hour. Suppose you know at 03:03 p.m., that your meeting shall go for next ninety minutes and you shall not be able to practice self-centering at 04:04 p.m. then intend for the future for the next 2 hours.

Add more steps or modify the steps to suit you. As an example, you may additionally pray for world peace at 9.09 a.m. or 9.09 p.m. Join lakhs of seekers who have signed up to pray for world peace at these two times (a Tejgyan Global Foundation initiative). Thousands of seekers have also reported that when they began practicing self-centering at unique times such as 01:01, 02:02, it was much easier for them to remember to do it. Generally saying that I will do it every hour has not proven to be as helpful. However, if you forget to practice self-centering at say 06:06 and you remember at 06:30, then practice self-centering the moment you remember. Do get back to the schedule at 07.07.

Akin to associating spiritual habits with what you are doing or at unique times, you may also perform a spiritual practice (*Sadhana*) whenever you feel negative emotions. And above all, always remember who you truly are whenever possible. By repeating these tiny habits, you are rewiring your spiritual neural pathways. With time, they will become highways which will help you efficiently progress on your spiritual path.

4

Want to Overcome Fear?

Learn the Lesson of Courage

People have different kinds of fears. Some people fear what is in the unknown such as future, death, darkness, old age, God, etc. Some are fearful of places such as heights, closed places, etc. There are some who fear the uncertainties in nature such as wild animals, fire, storms, lightening, earthquakes, etc. Some fear people like teachers, doctors, the opposite sex, famous people, strangers, boss, etc. There are some who have stage fright. And then there are those who are fearful of blood and some may be even afraid of drowning. One may wonder whether he or she needs to work on all sorts of fears in order to become completely free from fear. If you understand what fear does in your brain, you can use it to overcome any phobia. A phobia is an unwanted fear. However, necessary fears such as the fear of falling or fear of noise are not phobias.

 **Brain Research**

When we sense a scary stimulus, our body considers it to be an alarming situation. Our brain releases chemicals and within no time, we could develop physiological symptoms such as increase in heart rate, heavy breathing, perspiration, etc. Further, our pupils may dilate to let in more light, we may start feeling dizzy or light headed, our limbs may start trembling, there may be a churning in our stomach, etc. At such times, we choose to either fight, flight or freeze depending upon the way neural pathways are formed in our brain.

 Practical Application

If you want to get rid of fear, you need to change your neural pathways. You can do it by using any of these ways:

1. Make a physical change: Every time you are afraid, you may drink water or take a deep breath to rewire your brain. You can even try to exercise or go for a walk. The idea is to defocus your mind from the phobia and create a new neural pathway using a physical activity.

2. Laugh at your fear: By doing so, you diffuse the feelings associated with your fear and become comfortable with the object of fear. If you are afraid of a cockroach, tell yourself, "I am afraid of such a small creature. What can it do to me? Yet I am afraid. Ha! Ha! Ha!" By repeatedly doing this, a time will come when you become comfortable with cockroaches.

3. Use logical or rational thinking: If you are afraid of losing your job, tell yourself, "I am doing my job wholeheartedly, so nothing can happen to me. If at all I am dismissed from my job, my expertise and experience can fetch me any other job. So, nothing to worry about."

4. Use the law of average to take an overview of factual data related to your fear. If you are afraid of travelling by train fearing the possibility of an accident, gather the facts: how many times do trains run on that route in a year? How many accidents take place in a year? What are the chances of accidents occurring in a train you are travelling in? Invariably you may find that it's a minimal percentage of cases where it turns out to be true. With this, you can then be assured of your safe journey.

5. Repeat an affirmation such as, "I am God's property, no evil can touch me." If you are afraid of travelling alone at night and on an occasion if you do have to travel, repeat this mantra. Imagine white light around yourself with the faith that you have been protected by divine power.

The key idea here is to use any of the above ways to create a neural pathway and then face the fear. If you are afraid of darkness, either drink some water, or laugh at the fear, or use the law of average, or say an affirmation, and then venture out into darkness even if you are feeling fearful. A new neural pathway fused with the action of what you were fearful about is the key. And then repeat this action. Venture out into darkness a few more times. When you do so repeatedly, the new neural pathway will take over and you will no longer feel fearful. That is why it is said, "Face the fear and do it anyway."

✿ Spiritual Insight

You can spiritually rewire your neural pathways and get rid of fear too. The best way to do that is through mindfulness by witnessing the fear. The moment fear arises, observe how the body is reacting to the fear. Watch the fear mindfully. This is the fourth "f", "focus," other than the usual flight, fight, or freeze response.

There are some very deeply set fears in the depths of our minds arising out of trauma, setbacks, wrong programming since our childhood. Whenever these emotions arise, we either try to suppress them or express them in order to escape from the uncomfortable feelings. We may feel relieved with our escape mechanisms but the relief is temporary as the fear recurs again. Being consumed by these fears, some people tend to mentally experience a "mini death" every day.

You need not die every day before your actual death. When such fears get triggered, don't suppress them or express them according to your past conditioning. Just witness their rise and fall with the attitude of detachment and evenness backed by higher understanding. With true detached witnessing, an entire bunch of related emotions can be uprooted and released, just as we can uproot a bunch of weeds using a single weed as a hook. Our bodies get cleansed when these emotions are released. In the process, we experience healing from the traumas and setbacks that had held us. Situations that arise in our day-to-day life serve as opportunities for us to observe the deep-set emotions that get triggered within us. If these situations involve people, it helps to remember that these people are only being co-creators in our journey of cleansing ourselves off these dormant emotions that arise to the surface.

The understanding that you need to bear in mind is that these emotions are with your body-mind and not with the one who you truly are. You are the Source, Self, Consciousness who is using this body-mind as a medium to know itself and express its divine qualities. Whatever happens at the level of the body-mind is temporary. Hence, these emotions are also temporary; they come and go. They have arisen only to be released and present you with opportunities to express courage. Hence, learn to courageously face them instead of giving them undue importance or reacting to them indiscriminately.

As you repeatedly give new response, you help in strengthening the new neural pathway. Gradually, the new pathway will become a highway and slowly the old pathway will wane away.

Just like fear, we get overpowered by other emotions like anger, boredom, confusion, depression, envy, guilt, hatred, ill-will and jealousy. We already have neural pathways formed in our brain triggering these emotions. Some of these pathways were formed out of ignorance in our childhood. We unconsciously formed them by observing our parents and surroundings. Because of their repetition, our brain has assumed them to be our default behavior.

As we gain higher understanding and feel the urge to imbibe divine qualities, we need to change our responses to everyday situations in favor of these divine qualities. The more we repeat what we want in our life, the more we strengthen the new neural pathways. When our feelings, thoughts, speech and action are harmonized, nature also supports in strengthening the new neural pathways. Very soon the divine qualities become a reality for us. These divine qualities help us in stabilizing in our true nature.

5

The Way to Get What You Want

Learn How to Focus Your Brain

Has it happened to you that you are considering to buy a particular brand of a vehicle and then wherever you go, it is the same brand and the same model you notice again and again? If not, many people say that this is what happens to them. This phenomenon can be traced back to a small part of our brain called Reticular Activating System (RAS) situated just above where the spinal cord terminates in the brain.

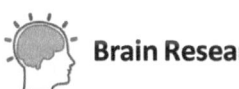 **Brain Research**

We receive massive information from our sensory organs but because of our brain's reticular activating system (RAS), only information which is of interest and important to us is filtered out for us. The RAS controls and directs our attention.

If someone calls you by your name from a distance, you can clearly hear it despite so many other sounds going around you. If you are driving a car, your whole focus is on driving. But as soon as your co-travelers discuss about a song, you immediately participate in it.

Thus, there will be so many objects around you but your focus will go on only those objects which interest you. More importantly, as you are singing a song with your co-travelers and suddenly another car is about to hit you from the front, it is your RAS that dims out all other information including who is singing and makes you focus only on the car that is in front of you so that you can avert an accident.

The RAS has two functions:

- It searches for data aligned to our beliefs, feelings, goals, and attitudes.
- It turns up the volume for anything that is valuable based on the above data or anything that is threatening.

 Practical Application

If you have been ignorant about the RAS functioning within you, you may have been unconscious about the inputs that have gone into your RAS so far. Accordingly, your RAS has filtered information that was emotionally important to you or aligned with your beliefs. Consequently, it has shown you the world in terms of these inputs, causing you to attract the same in your life. Now you can consciously put your desired goals (what you want to achieve) into your RAS so that your brain automatically focuses on that and brings it into your life. To change your life, change the inputs given to RAS.

RAS looks for pictures with emotional intensity repeated multiple times across many days. Thus, you need to take care of three things: intensity, frequency and duration. Thus, whatever you want in life see it happening passionately (emotional intensity), see it many times in a day (frequency) and see it for a few weeks (duration). In a short period, your RAS will begin responding to the pictures you are giving it.

If you want any quality within you, say confidence, then say an affirmation such as "I am confident" repeatedly, passionately and consistently.

As seen in the picture below, you need to amplify some thoughts (your goals) repeatedly so that the RAS can understand this is different than other random thoughts.

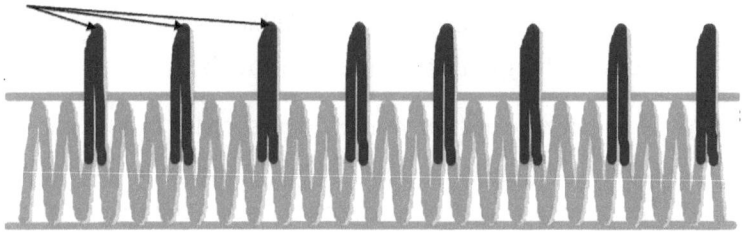

🪷 Spiritual Insight

You can use the power of the RAS for your spiritual growth too. Here are some ways to do so:

1. If you are enslaved by negative defilements like anger, boredom, depression, fear, guilt, hatred, ill-will, jealousy, you can become free from them by using the power of the RAS. Instead of focusing on the negative traits, focus on the positive qualities such as love, joy, peace, courage, creativity, confidence, devotion, gratitude, patience. Reaffirm and reinforce to yourself that there is abundance of all these qualities within you. You may write down how your life

will be after you have inculcated these positive qualities in your life. Repeatedly affirm to yourself that you are in favor of these qualities and are loving them. Gradually, it will get programmed into your RAS and you will become a magnet for these qualities.

2. Your core thoughts and beliefs play an important role in shaping your life. If you want to change the quality of your life, identify your core thoughts and beliefs. Imbibe the new thoughts and beliefs which will help you bring your envisioned life into reality. Thus, using your spiritual understanding, change your beliefs. As your beliefs become aligned to a divine life, the RAS will start showing you more of those things that are aligned to your beliefs.

3. You can take help of your RAS to speed up your progress on the spiritual path. If you have pictures symbolizing your life purpose and associated spiritual goals, then look at them frequently during the course of the day for many days with the faith that they will soon come into fruition.

6

How to Handle Uncomfortable Feelings?

Learn to Escape from Escapism

We all have feelings. More often than not, what we dread are uncomfortable feelings. Let's look at some examples:

a. Imagine, you have been busy with lots of activities and suddenly there is no activity. How would you feel then?

b. You have been fired from work. You reach home and the house is full of guests. How would you feel then?

c. Despite you working hard, your colleague got recognition and you were not acknowledged. How would you feel?

d. On a quiet Sunday when you are sitting at home alone, all of a sudden a sad memory from the past pops up in your mind and you become sad. What would you do then?

e. You call for a meeting and no one turns up. How would you feel?

f. One of your aspiring clients calls off his business and all your future plans crumble. How would you feel?

g. You take out time from your busy schedule and go for a family function. No one attends to you there. How would you feel?

It is observed that in most of the above mentioned scenarios, one feels uncomfortable. We either shut down the emotion by suppressing it or find a temporary way of escaping it by diverting focus to topics that provide temporary relief. One may switch on the TV, call a friend, chat with someone, surf on the net, go for eating out, take a walk, express one's anger, etc. So what happens in the brain when it comes to these uncomfortable feelings?

 Brain Research

In everyday language we often use the terms feelings and emotions interchangeably as they are closely associated with each other. We are constantly contacting the external world through our senses. Our brain is receiving signals from the body, registering what is going on inside our body. Emotions are the complex reactions the body has to certain stimuli.

When a situation that we have associated with fear occurs, it triggers various body sensations. Our hearts begin to race, our mouths become dry, our skin turns pale and our muscles contract. These sensations form a physical snapshot in the brain. This physical snapshot is triggered automatically and unconsciously whenever the situation is repeated. When the brain interprets the situation as one of fear, it triggers this emotional reaction that leads to the physical symptoms.

However, not all feelings result from the body's reaction to external stimuli. Sometimes, we see a sick person and empathize with him.

At such times, we simulate the pain in our brain. Without actually experiencing the pain physically, we recreate that person's pain to a certain degree internally.

Sometimes, the physical snapshot is also not accurate as the brain ignores certain physical signals when the body goes through severe stress or severe fear. Thus, sometimes the brain doesn't receive the accurate snapshot of the physical state and misinterprets the feeling. At other times, even though it receives the correct snapshot, it still misinterprets the feeling. It may blow up the intensity and severity of a feeling to such an extent that it is as if a panic button has been pressed. At times, the entire body starts trembling with fear. If it senses an uncomfortable feeling, it tries to do away with it. It prompts the body to act in such a way that it escapes from the uncomfortable situation.

From childhood, whatever we have believed to be true is stored in our brain. These beliefs are nothing but the neural pathways which decide how the brain should interpret the emotions, which feelings should be generated and how to respond to them. Accordingly, the brain directs the body to behave in a particular way. It's like all of them are wired together and fire together.

If the brain is faced with an emotion which doesn't match with the set belief system, then instead of reporting that it doesn't know how to interpret this emotion, it replays any of the existing feelings like anger, boredom, comparison, disgust, depression, envy, fear, guilt, hatred, ill-will, jealousy. Our physical state also changes accordingly. The brain releases chemicals along the neural pathway and the symptoms are shown on different parts of the body.

For every emotion, different parts of the body get affected. For example, when the feeling of anger arises in a body, the brain releases stress hormones in the body. It shunts blood away from the gut and towards the muscles, in preparation for physical exertion. Heart rate, blood pressure and respiration increase, the body temperature rises and the skin perspires.

As we see it, we believe in it and reinforce the emotion. As the brain automates these responses, you will not be consciously aware of them to take the corrective actions. At such times, instead of masking the underlying emotion, you need to fully feel it and face it. As you re-evaluate it, you understand its real worth. Then you need to give clear inputs to the brain on how to process this information. Thus, a new neural pathway will get formed with the renewed response.

 Practical Application

Whenever you experience an uncomfortable feeling, understand that your brain is not able to process the information properly. You need to give correct inputs to your brain in order to harbor positive feelings such as love, joy, peace, patience, courage, compassion, etc. Let's now revisit the above example scenarios again in light of this understanding.

1. If you have been busy with lots of activities and suddenly there is no activity, then you may feel a void within. Your brain will interpret it as a feeling of boredom and may want to indulge in activities such as chatting, shopping, eating out, etc. At such time, understand that as you have not given correct inputs to your brain, it's resorting to these avenues. When such feeling arises you need to tell your brain to behave differently. You may practice meditation and become aware

of the exact physical state. One of the best meditations for emotions is to watch your breath. As you focus on your breath, your breathing calms down and the effect of the emotion reduces too.

2. You have been fired from work. You reach home and the house is full of guests. At such a time, you would have loved to be with yourself. But when you see the guests around, your brain doesn't understand how to interpret this feeling, and you can get frustrated and avoid the situation. At such times, you could have just watched your emotions and re-evaluated its worth. That would have helped you in being patient in that situation.

3. Despite you working hard, your colleague got recognition and you were not acknowledged. The reward center in your brain is already activated to receive the recognition. The neural pathway is triggered and you crave for the recognition. Suddenly, when you see your colleague got all the recognition, your brain interprets it as an unwelcome situation and fires anger through the neural pathway. However, you should understand that you could have given a different response without showing anger. You could have chosen to rejoice your friend's appreciation. By doing this, you get tuned with the positive vibrations and some day you too will get recognized. By being angry, you get into negative vibrations.

4. On a quiet Sunday when you are sitting at home alone, all of a sudden a sad memory from the past pops up in your mind and you become sad. At that time, you feel it's right to become sad. However, by being unhappy you reinforce the seeds of unhappiness for your future. Instead, you can

also choose to be happy. By being happy, you program your brain to handle such kind of situations in future.

5. You call for a meeting and no one turns up. You may feel disgusted at such a time. By feeling that way, you only trouble yourself. Rather than controlling what others should do, first control your emotions. Be happy regardless of how the situation is. By being happy you respect yourself.

6. One of your aspiring clients calls off his business and all your future plans crumble. You may feel disappointed and depressed at such a time. Your body will also start showing symptoms accordingly. However, you can still choose to accept the situation and relax. Feel yourself fully. Once the feelings subside then with a calm mind you can think about the best possible solution and start working on it.

7. You take out time from your busy schedule and go for a family function. No one attends to you over there. You feel left out or ignored. You grumble on your decision to be there. You feel instead of being there, you could have focused on completing some of your priority tasks. Question yourself if you were given proper attention, would such thoughts have arisen in your mind? They wouldn't. So, this is the neural pathway in your brain which is triggering this action. The brain has misinterpreted your emotions; hence such feeling has arisen. It was your decision to be there. The happiness you experienced while taking that decision can still continue. Your happiness is not dependent upon any external factors. With this declaration, you will feel happy. Your happiness may attract others towards you but that's a bonus.

As you change your feelings, your brain gets rewired with the new programming and the same situations will open a new door of possibilities for you.

🪷 Spiritual Insight

An uncomfortable feeling not only comes from the external stimuli but it also arises from within as a result of change in mood, memory and surroundings. Whenever we face an uncomfortable feeling, we may either explode or suppress it within. When we spew it out on others, it results into anger, hatred and envy binding us into a karmic bondage. The other person tries to search for an opportunity to get even with us. Thus, we may temporarily safeguard our physical health by expressing anger or resentment on others, but it is at the cost of harmony in our relations. Ultimately it leads us to regret.

Conversely, when we suppress the feeling within, we may appear calm from outside but internally we simmer. If we continue to suppress it for a long time, one fine day it becomes unbearable and we explode like a volcano. When feelings are suppressed for long, they lead to various kinds of illnesses. Studies have shown that such suppressed feelings affect various parts of the body. For example, fear can affect the kidneys and the urinary bladder, hatred can affect the lungs, guilt can affect the neck, depression can affect the feet, too much of emotional burden can cause the shoulder pain.

Instead of suppressing or exploding our feelings, there is a third way of witnessing them from a detached standpoint. This detached witnessing consists of three aspects:

1. Understanding – As we saw above, every emotion resides in specific parts of the body. When an emotion arises, the

respective neural pathway activates corresponding parts of the body. Thus, we start sensing that emotion on our body. Looking at the physical snapshot, our brain determines the corresponding feeling. As you observe the emotion, you believe that it's happening with you. Hence, you find it difficult to detach from it.

However, you need to understand that the emotions are with your body-mind, not with you. Who you truly are is separate from the body-mind. As you understand this, it becomes easy to detach from the emotions. Further, you need to understand that every emotion arises, sustains for some time and then subsides. Thus, it is temporary just like a wave in an ocean. It will arise and then subside. If you witness it, you will become free from it. The next time when the emotion arises, you will not experience it as severe. Thus, as you watch it as a detached witness with this understanding, gradually its effect will diminish. Soon you will find that you are able to maintain poise in the same situations where you used to get troubled earlier.

Let's understand this with the help of an example. For a snake to shed its old outgrown skin, it has to rub itself against rough surfaces. It goes through a lot of pain. But when it comes out of it, it gets a brand new skin. Similarly, when you go through uncomfortable feelings, understand that they have arisen to release your potential. Thus, when you go through fearful feelings, tell yourself that God is taking care of you. Your mind will then become quiet. As you witness the feeling of fear from a detached standpoint, all your residual fears also get uprooted along with this emotion and slowly you emerge as a courageous winner. If you have hatred against someone and you witness this emotion from a detached standpoint, compassion will automatically arise within you.

However, if you lack the right understanding, your mind will try to do away with the feeling by escaping and instigate you to indulge in shopping, chatting, browsing, eating something, etc. If you have an uncomfortable feeling on your body, you may take medicine. With this, you may feel relieved and relaxed but it's all temporary. After some period, you will again have the same feeling. Hence instead of escaping to other resorts, witness your feelings with the right understanding and soon you will be free from them.

2. Equanimity – The other aspect of detached witnessing is equanimity. Equanimity is all about seeing painful and pleasurable emotions alike without craving or aversion. When you see things from equanimity, you experience a sense of evenness where there is neither a like nor a dislike for what is being witnessed.

In case of emotions such as anger, depression, or resentment, looking at the physical snapshot, our brain misinterprets them and ascribes an exaggerated weight to them. As a result, we feel heavy and intense. When we slow down and watch the emotion with an attitude of equanimity, we are able to question the weight of the emotion. What may appear to be a heavyweight emotion, of the order of magnitude of say 50 kg, will then turn out to be not even the magnitude of 5 grams. This is the revelation that can result out of deep observation with equanimity.

3. Alertness – Being vigilant is essential to remain detached. When we are not alert, the natural tendency is to identify with the emotion and create further stories about it in the mind. We need to have an alert awareness that is uncompromisingly focused on itself. It vigilantly utilizes emotions that arise as hooks to defocus from what arises and refocus on our essential Presence, i.e. who we truly are.

Using these three aspects, when you witness emotions from a detached standpoint, your old neural pathways will get replaced with new ones. You will be able to maintain your calm in situations where you used to get angry. You will not get troubled by problems as much. Instead, you will choose to respond to problems instead of reacting to them, thus making problems a stepping stone for your progress. Thus, you will no longer escape from situations.

7

Placebo Effect – Nocebo Effect

As You Believe, So Shall You Experience.

Before we discuss brain research on placebo and nocebo effects, let us look at some examples.

a. Example 1: When American surgeon Henry Beecher was treating wounded American soldiers during World War II, he ran out of pain-killing morphine. He was desperate to help them. So, in place of morphine, he injected them with a saline solution. To his surprise, the solution worked as a pain-killer for 40% of soldiers and he could operate on them successfully. How could these soldiers endure the intolerable pain with a saline solution?

b. Example 2: A person believed that he suffered from motion sickness. As soon as he would feel the motion of the vehicle, he would feel dizzy, nauseated and the churning of his stomach. When he took a pill, he would immediately feel relieved. On one such occasions he was given a plain sugar pill instead of his usual pill and he still felt better. What made him feel better on this occasion?

c. Example 3: A person attending an evening party encountered a lady who had adorned her hair with flowers. Seeing the flower on the lady, he got into a sneezing bout as he was allergic to this flower. He continued to sneeze and pointed towards her hair. The lady plucked a flower from her hair and showed him that it was made of plastic. He was at once, miraculously cured! What made him sneeze in the first place? And what *cured* him?

d. Example 4: A healthy man went for a health check-up. Due to some technical or human error, his reports got exchanged with that of a cancer patient. He read that his cancer was at the last stage and he would not survive beyond six months. He fully believed it and soon developed symptoms of dizziness, memory loss, weakness, weight loss, etc. He started counting his last days. As he was wasting away, he had to be admitted to a hospital due to multiple health complications. All the tests were conducted again. Everyone was astonished to know that he never had cancer to begin with. The disease which supposedly made him suffer, was not there at all. Why then did he suffer?

e. Example 5: An experiment was conducted on two people who suffered from headaches. The first one was given a pain-killing medicine and the second one was given a sugar pill. They were told the same too. However, while administering those pills they were interchanged without their notice. The sugar pill was enclosed in the garb of a pain-killer and the pain-killer was given as a sugar pill. Now, the person who took the sugar pill in the garb of the pain killer immediately felt relieved of the pain whereas the other one still suffered from headache thinking that the sugar pill couldn't cure him. What caused these diametrically opposite results?

 Brain Research

If we believe in something or anticipate some outcome, our expectation induces an active stimulus in our brain and it releases chemicals accordingly. It affects the cells of our body including the brain. Sometimes, our genes can also get affected due to our beliefs. It can cause a therapeutic change in our behavior, experience, or physiology.

Our beliefs also result in the formation of neural pathways in our brain. Every belief has a behavior and a feeling associated with it and has its own neural pathway. The association of every belief, feeling and behavior is stored in our memory as a mental fusion. Whatever is wired together, fires together. Hence, whenever we repeat the belief, the associated feeling and behavior also repeat in turn, making us experience it in the same way every time. The more we have faith in the belief, the more evidence we get and the belief gets all the more reinforced. With every repetition, it becomes a stronger neural highway.

The good news is that by merely changing our beliefs, we can witness change in our feelings and behavior in the original scenario. As we saw in the first example in this chapter, the soldiers believed that they were injected with a pain-killer instead of a mere saline solution, hence they could endure the intolerable pain. Thus, new neural pathways got created for this new mental fusion. Whenever the new belief is repeated, the brain releases different chemicals which in turn cause desired changes in the body cells. With constant repetition, the neural pathway becomes a highway!

Depending upon the belief induced in the brain, anticipated results are experienced in the body. If the belief is positive, the results will be positive and vice versa. The Placebo effect and the Nocebo effect are based on these principles. They have been widely used in psychology and medicine.

The phenomenon, in which the recipient perceives an improvement in condition due to positive expectations, rather than the treatment itself, is known as the placebo effect or the placebo response. The phenomenon, in which the recipient's condition worsens due to his negative expectations, rather than treatment or causative ingredient is called the nocebo effect.

Placebo is a substance or treatment with no active therapeutic effect. Common placebos include sugar pills, saline water, etc. They are commonly used in cases involving pain, depression, anxiety, fatigue, etc. As we saw in the above examples, people were cured when they were administered a placebo medicine.

- In example 1, the saline solution acted as a placebo. The soldiers could endure pain because they strongly believed the saline solution to be a pain killer. Thus, even though they were not injected with a pain killer, their positive belief helped them to endure the severe pain successfully.
- In example 2, the pill acted as a placebo. The person's strong belief about having motion sickness made him feel dizzy and nauseated. But as soon as he gulped the pill, he felt better. The pill worked in his favor because he strongly believed that the pill would cure him.

- In example 3, when the person realized that the flower was fake, his belief changed immediately, and so did his experience. Consequently, he felt better.
- In example 5, the person gulped a sugar pill in the garb of a pain-killer. He believed that the pain killer would give him relief and the belief worked. He got cured of his headache. The sugar pill acted as a placebo for him.

The Nocebo effect is when a negative outcome is observed in life as a result of negative beliefs and expectations. The nocebo effect is illustrated in examples 3, 4 and 5.

- In example 3, the person believed that the flower was real. Hence, the allergic symptoms associated with the belief were felt on his body and soon he felt dizzy.
- In example 4, the healthy person believed that he had cancer. Hence, his body immediately threw up the symptoms of cancer, even though there was no cancer.
- In example 5, the person believed the pain-killer to be a sugar pill. He believed that a sugar pill cannot cure him and his belief nullified the effect of the pain-killer. As a result, he didn't experience relief from his headache.

 Practical Application

If you want to change your life, you need to change your beliefs. You need to inculcate new positive healthy beliefs, which will in turn act as a placebo. The more you repeat these belief statements passionately and frequently with faith and feeling, the more strength they gain to manifest into reality. Harmony in your feelings, thoughts, speech and action boosts these beliefs to manifest in your life. Very soon repetition of these positive healthy beliefs will change the blueprint of your brain. The cells of your body including the brain can change. Your genes too can change. Attaining physical fitness, mental peace, social harmony, financial abundance and spiritual wellbeing will not become farfetched for you.

For example, suppose that you tell yourself, "Whenever I eat yogurt, I become more healthy." Research proves that even if you know that this is a placebo, it will still produce the desired result.

Recent scientific research explains how the human DNA can be influenced and reprogrammed by words and frequencies without the need for intervention in the physical plane. Only 10% of our DNA is used for building proteins. Till recently, the other 90% was considered "junk DNA." However, recent collaborative research by linguists and geneticists discovered that the apparently useless 90% of the human DNA is not only responsible for constructing our bodies but also serves as means for data storage and communication. It contains encoded data that follows the same grammar rules of syntax and semantics as our human languages. So the evolution of human languages is not a coincidence, but rather a reflection of our inherent DNA. Due to this, human DNA resonates with human language.

So it turns out that we can use words and sentences of human language to influence living DNA! This has been experimentally proven. DNA present in living tissue responds to language-modulated inputs. This scientifically explains why affirmations and auto-suggestions have such strong effects on our bodies and physiology. Spiritually evolved humans have known for ages that our body is programmable by language, words and thought. This is now gaining scientific ground.

In order to repeat these positive belief statements, you may write them down in your notebook and read them aloud. You may repeat them in a relaxed posture, either sitting on a chair or lying down on the bed. The potency of spoken words increases manifold when your body is relaxed. When you repeat these statements with faith and love, they get instilled in your mind immediately. You may also sing them to yourself in a lulling tone. Melody and harmony are infallible catalysts for creating deep positive impressions in the mind.

Also become aware of the nocebo effect. Is your negative expectation creating a negative outcome? For instance, are you telling yourself, "I am getting old, so I am losing enthusiasm"? If this is the case, tell yourself that you are falling prey to the nocebo effect and that your physical age has nothing to do with your mental age.

🪷 Spiritual Insight

Since our childhood, we have nurtured fixed beliefs by observing our parents, friends, neighborhood and the media. We have believed them without questioning their authenticity. By reading or watching news, we have believed that the same will happen with us as well. We might have started living a constricted life that is full of fear, uncertainty and insecurity. Many believe that life will be like this forever and therefore it manifested into reality. Our beliefs created the world we live in now. If we are experiencing discontentment, sorrow and failure, it is because these beliefs have acted as a nocebo in our lives. Most people believe that their life situations and people are the culprit for their miseries and try hard to correct them. But to no avail.

When you question these deep-seated beliefs, you may find that they are no longer valid. The truth may be completely different. You need to rethink your beliefs and command your body that it can completely heal itself by releasing these beliefs that do not serve you. It is possible to be free from all such core beliefs. It is not a sugar pill that cures you, but the change in your thoughts. Knowing this, you can have faith that just by changing your thoughts, you can also heal yourself. If you experience that the same situations are repeating in life, then it is only because the same thoughts have been unconsciously repeated within you.

Once you identify the limiting beliefs within you, you can replace them with new positive thoughts, which align with love, joy, peace and harmony. Whenever negative beliefs come into play, instruct yourself that you don't need them now and can delete them. If you have been in their favor, you can firmly resolve to be in favor of positive beliefs, which will have positive healing effect in your life. Soon you will see that new reality will manifest. For example, if you were harboring hatred for someone due to your old belief, you will feel compassion for the same person due to your changed positive belief. Thus, despite the situation being the same, just by changing your beliefs, your experience can change.

Beyond Placebo and Nocebo

As you experiment with positive beliefs and begin to see a positive transformation, you can consider breaking free from the cocoon of all your limited beliefs. But for that, you need to learn to see the truth as it is without being swayed by a placebo or a nocebo. Then you will be free from the influence of all the placebos and nocebos in your life. In fact, the greatest nocebo is that we have forgotten who we truly are. We have believed ourselves to be limited individuals, thereby living a constricted life. But as we begin to experientially know our true nature, the true Self or Pure Consciousness, we become completely free from this illusion.

When you have the firm understanding that all the beliefs are with your body and mind, not with you, that who you truly are is separate from them, then you can watch their effect on your body-mind with equanimity and alertness. With every response that arises from a belief, you will see it arise, stay for some time, and then dissolve. You will recognize the temporary nature of the play of these beliefs. As you consistently watch this rise and fall, they will dissolve gradually.

As you lead a life free of beliefs and tendencies, you will experience joy in the midst of all circumstances. Thereafter, the infinite latent potential of the true Self begins to express through your body-mind. You start leading a fresh life of abundance, health, wealth, harmony, joy, creativity and positivity. A life, free from beliefs, is a stress-free life, where everything happens spontaneously in perfection. Even if few people bring it out into practice, they can bring about a positive change in the world.

8

Delayed Gratification

Change Your Focus

In the 1960's, psychologist Walter Mischel performed an experiment with a group of children in the age group of four to six years. They were led into an empty room with no distractions. They were offered a choice between eating one piece of their favorite marshmallow immediately or eat two pieces of marshmallow after twenty minutes. The tester left the room and returned after twenty minutes.

He observed three different categories of behaviors:

a. In the first category, children couldn't resist their temptation and immediately ate the marshmallow as soon as the tester left the room.

b. In the second category, children were waiting for twenty minutes but all the time their focus was on the marshmallow. They somehow tried to control themselves from eating. But, they couldn't stop themselves from smelling it. They tried their best to shift their focus away from it but couldn't help seeing it from the corner of their eyes. In their desperation they pulled their hair and did various things in anticipation of getting two pieces after twenty minutes. Waiting for twenty minutes became a torture for them.

c. In the third category, children were happily waiting for twenty minutes by diverting their focus away from the marshmallow and doing something creative during the wait.

When they followed up the same children as grown-ups after many years, they found that the children who couldn't resist their temptation couldn't become as successful as those who could. Those who could delay their gratification became proficient and attained success in their life. Their success was measured in terms of academic progress, physical fitness, social harmony and mental stability. Based on this experiment, it was concluded that those who could delay their gratification during school-days attained success as a grown-up. Those who fell prey to their temptations couldn't go very far in their career.

 Brain Research

Our brain has a rewarding system which consists of a group of neural structures responsible for generating craving or pleasure upon receiving a specific stimulus. The stimulus can be any object, event, activity or situation which has the potential to make us approach and consume it. When exposed to such a stimulus, our brain generates chemicals and the neural pathway of the reward system gets activated. The craving forces us to approach that object and consume it. The more we consume it, the more craving our brain develops in response to the chemicals generated and the neural pathway gets strongly reinforced. Later it becomes difficult to control the temptation as it was seen in the first category of behavior.

In the second and the third category of behavior, because of the positive reinforcement of receiving two pieces of marshmallow, the children were motivated to learn a new behavior. They developed power to delay their gratification. They resisted their temptation for instant gratification and could wait for a bigger delayed reward. Their new behavior created a new neural pathway. However, in case of second category, as the children intermittently kept their focus on the marshmallow, the sight of the marshmallow generated craving within them. The more they saw it, the more it reinforced the craving and finally they either smelled it or touched it.

In case of the third category, those children completely diverted their focus to something different than the object of craving. As a result, their new neural pathway became stronger and they could keep themselves away from the marshmallow.

As these children grew up, repetition of this behavior reinforced their habits which played an important role in their achievements later in their life. Those who could delay instant gratification could complete their education and had better paying jobs as adults than those who exhibited a lesser degree of self-control.

 Practical Application

The modern world is one of instant gratification. From Mobile Apps to e-commerce, all are pushing us towards instant gratification. You can instantly download what you want to watch. Messaging apps like WhatsApp instantly deliver and are constantly pulling your senses. Rather, you allow them to pull your senses. Practice delayed gratification instead of instant gratification in such cases. When you wish to reach out to your phone to see what the latest message is all about, you can say to yourself, "Let me see this after I do some work." Put it off till you can by changing your focus. You may see it when you finish doing the work you decided to do or you may see it at a fixed time every day. By delaying indulgence towards your senses, you are building the muscle of delayed gratification.

Many people misunderstand the practical application of the Marshmallow experiment for delayed gratification. They think that it is all about will power and that will power is short in supply. The often-missed learning from the Marshmallow experiment is that instead of fighting your will like the second category of children did, it is better to change your focus like the third category of children. Changing your focus when you want to engage in a dysfunctional habit by doing something creative and focusing on a new neural pathway is a powerful tool. Here are some practical applications of the same:

1. People like sportsmen, athletes, singers, film artists, etc., can make use of this research to delay their gratifications for the attainment of their larger goal. Doing creative things when they would like to instantly gratify their senses or visualizing the vision and recalling their larger goal can help them. Consequently, their goal driven efforts will pay off when they achieve success later.

2. Those who want to get rid of their smoking or drinking habit can use this research. Every time they want to smoke or consume alcohol, if they see a picture of throat cancer or of a damaged liver in their minds, these two stimuli will get wired together in their brain. Thus, whenever they will think of smoking they will be reminded of the picture and soon

they will quit smoking. Alternatively, they can do something creative whenever they feel the urge to smoke.

3. This research can help people who want to lose weight. When there is craving for high calorie food, they can delay their gratification by attaching a painful image to this. Thus, high calorie food and avoidance will be wired together. This will create a new pathway in their brain. Slowly, they will avoid immediately eating high calorie favorite food resulting in losing their weight.

Alternatively, they can also visualize a picture of their non-favorite healthy low calorie food and see the picture of their slim, trim and fit body. The sight of the low calorie healthy food which didn't generate any craving in them will now be pleasing and they will consume it happily. They will be encouraged to eat this healthy food and lose weight, gain a slim, trim and fit-body in turn.

Again, doing something creative or something that one enjoys is also a powerful way to handle food cravings.

4. Many a time, people don't have harmony in their relations due to their impulsive behavior. Their mind forces them to quickly retaliate the other person which lands them in trouble. By delaying gratification through change of focus, they can harmonize their relations. Next time you feel like lashing out at a friend or a relative, take a walk, drink a glass of water, listen to a song. Change your focus and practice delayed gratification easily.

Every time your senses demand indulgence, engage yourself into some activity, no matter however tiny it may be. By delaying gratification through change of focus, you are slowly erasing the existing neural pathway and creating a new one.

🪷 Spiritual Insight

The tendency to gratify our senses is an impediment in spiritual growth. By serving our senses we serve our ego. When we indiscriminately indulge in our senses, we get sidetracked from our spiritual path. However, if we train ourselves on self-control and delay gratification of our senses through change of focus, it helps to build our spiritual power. The joy we will experience thereafter will be much more superior than the pleasure we would have derived by gratifying our senses. Thus, we opt for the more fulfilling reward that comes later, instead of the immediate reward that seems more compelling. Thereafter, the same senses can become instrumental for serving the highest desire of the Self and we can progress on our spiritual path to attain Self-realization and Self-stabilization.

With this understanding about delayed gratification, while practicing meditation, when you feel compelled to react, you can delay the urge to respond. With time you will find that the compulsive or impulsive nature of the mind diminishes. When your defilements try to overpower you, delay their gratification. For example, if you feel like shouting at someone, delay it. If you are bored and your senses want to indulge in some entertainment or food, delay it. If you want to indulge in worrying about something, delay it. If you feel sad and dejected, delay it. By delaying the gratification of your defilements, you get freedom to choose what you are in favor of. With consistent practice, you remain happy amidst all circumstances of your life.

Here are a few spiritual tools to change your focus that will help in delayed gratification:

1. Mindfulness is a powerful way to change your focus that helps in delayed gratification. Instead of focusing on the object of gratification, focus on your breath or the sensations of your body. Be mindful of what is happening to them. Notice what is happening in the present moment.
2. Change your focus by changing the question you ask yourself. Instead of asking, "Should I indulge or not", ask yourself, "Is it a need or a want?" If it's the want of the senses, you can hold back your desire. You can experiment with other questions such as, "Can I accept not indulging in this?"
3. Devotion is another way to change your focus. Change your focus to God instead of the object of gratification. Sing praise of God, marvel at the beauty of creation or practice chanting to change your focus.
4. Every time you are compelled to respond in the usual habitual way, you can delay it by taking a meditative pause. This pause will allow you to exercise a freedom of choice. This new response in turn will create a new neural pathway and you will get liberated from your mechanical behavior.

9

Mirror Neurons

The Magic of Unseen Effect

If you stick your tongue out at a newborn, they may automatically stick out their tongue back at you. This is because their mirror neurons are firing and it helps them to imitate what they are seeing. Humans learn through watching and observing other humans. Mirror neurons are important for understanding the actions and intentions of other people, and for learning new skills by imitation. They are involved in planning and controlling actions, abstract thinking, and memory. Let us understand this through some examples:

- Have you ever felt happy after spending your time with babies?
- Have you felt totally drained after spending time with certain people?
- Have you felt inspired after listening to a motivational speaker or reading someone's biography?
- Have you felt terrified while watching a horror movie?

- Have you felt compassionate for someone after hearing their sad story?
- After reading some news about a road accident, did you ever get the feeling "this could have happened to me"?
- After watching your favorite actor's movie, when you walk out of the theatre, do you feel like imitating the actor? Does your body language change?

Assuming your answers is "yes" to many of these questions, know that all this happens because of mirror neurons.

 Brain Research

In early 1990, a group of neurophysiologists at the University of Parma, Italy, conducted research on the neurons specialized for the control of hand and mouth actions in Macaque monkeys. They observed that a class of neurons respond when the monkey performs actions like picking up food and when it observes another person picking up some food. The same neurons fire when the monkey rips off a piece of paper and when it sees a person rip off a paper, or hears a paper being ripped off (without visual cues). These class of neurons came to be known as mirror neurons.

Mirror neurons fire in both the cases: when an animal acts, or even while it observes the same action being performed by another. Thus, the neurons of the observer "mirrors" the behavior of the other, as though the observer were itself acting out the behavior. Based on these observations the researchers came to believe that mirror neurons encode abstract concepts of actions like ripping paper, picking up food, etc., whether the action is performed by the monkey or any other animal.

It is no surprise that mirror neurons are functional in humans too, as they have evolved biologically from the predecessors of apes. Also, should it then be a surprise that "aping" in English means "imitating"!?

Mirror neurons are thus a type of brain cells that fire either when you do a particular action, or when you simply watch someone else doing the same action. For example, when you pick up a glass and when you see someone else pick up a glass, the same neurons fire in your brain. If you hear someone eating an apple, some of the same neurons fire that do when you eat the apple yourself. They constantly fire and try to imitate whatever they see, hear or smell. They help in understanding the actions and intentions of other people, and for learning new skills by imitation. The mirror neuron system plays a key role in your ability to empathize, socialize, and communicate your emotions. How strongly your mirror neurons' system gets activated determines how empathetic you feel.

When you watch your favorite actor's movie, you may imitate the actor unknowingly after walking out of the theatre. Your body language may change. This can happen because your mirror neurons get activated while you watch the movie. They believe that you are physically performing the actor's role. For the same reason, you may feel terrified when you watch a horror movie. When you read some news about a road accident, you may believe the same could happen to you too. When you listen to a motivational speaker, or read a biography, you may feel inspired.

 Practical Application

Mirror neurons can prove to be a blessing if you utilize them to their fullest. They can be helpful in all spheres of activities.

1. If an athlete wants to gain expertise in his chosen field, he can watch experts performing in the field and emulate them. If he mentally rehearses the game, then that will also activate the same motor neurons required to perform fine-tuned motor skills. Thus, his mirror neurons will encode the action of the expert and believe as if he is physically performing it. Soon he will become an expert in his field. The same principle can also be used for other sports such as cricket, badminton, boxing, and even for dance choreography.

2. If someone wants to become an expert public speaker, he can watch the performances of doyens in that field. He can mentally rehearse their speeches and practice delivering the punch lines. With every repetition, his mirror neurons get activated. It happens as if he has physically delivered those speeches and soon he develops confidence and becomes a master in public speaking.

3. As we saw earlier, babies are masters when it comes to imitation. When they observe an action, the same neurons get activated that will be needed for the babies to perform the action themselves. The actions they see help them form connections in their brain allowing them to perform that action. Imitation in essence becomes a vital factor for babies to learn and develop. Mirror neurons make their task vastly easier. They enable the baby to learn, walk, talk, and behave like their parents or peers by emulating their actions and behavior.

When parents understand the principle of mirror neurons, they can raise their babies and build the qualities they want in their children. They can create a conducive atmosphere while nurturing their babies. They can ensure that they demonstrate the same qualities which they wish their children should imbibe. They can selectively choose an appropriate company and environment for the growth of their children.

4. The mirror neuron system helps us to decode (receive and interpret) facial expressions. Whether we are observing a specific expression or making it ourselves, the same regions of our brain get activated. The better we are at interpreting facial expressions, the more active our mirror neuron system is. You must have experienced that after seeing a smiling baby, you too smile back. If you spend time with people burdened with anxiety and stress, soon you too feel drained. It is possible that people who have more active mirror neurons can be experts in mimicry.

5. Have you ever watched a TV program where someone is crying and you find yourself brought to tears as well? Why does this happen to you? After all you didn't go through the suffering that the other person did. This happens because mirror neurons not only imitate external behavior but can also imitate internal behavior. In this case, you empathize with the other person's feelings.

Same applies when you are feeling lethargic and you happen to see an enthusiastic group of joggers, you too feel like jogging. While you are watching the last over of a cricket match on TV, you too experience the same tension and anxiety that the spectator is experiencing in the stadium. When your favorite team wins the match, you too rejoice like the spectators in the stadium. When your favorite player hits a century, you feel as happy as he is. Thus, the practical application when it comes to emotions is to see the emotions you would like in yourself in others to have the mirror neurons fire.

6. The studies from mirror neuron research are leading to new therapies for helping stroke victims to regain their lost movement. Using mirror therapy, a reflection of their unaffected arm is created in the place of their affected arm. The mirror image tricks their brain into thinking that their affected arm is moving like an unaffected arm. This triggers their mirror neurons to fire. This illusion helps their brain rewire itself through neuroplasticity. Even though it's just a reflection of their unaffected arm, studies have shown that their brain still perceives it as their affected arm and their mobility can improve.

7. When one has a poor self-image, mirror neurons can help in changing it by imitating or role modeling after a person who has all the positive qualities that one wants to inculcate.

Spiritual Insight

Having understood that mirror neurons can imitate whatever they see, you can put them to their best use for your spiritual growth. You may have heard the story of Ekalavya from the Mahabharata. Ekalavya, a son of a poor hunter, learnt archery from the statue of guru Dronacharya. What made him become an expert in archery? Apart from his loyalty, dedication and sincerity, mirror neurons helped him attain the mastery. He just got one opportunity to observe his guru teaching archery to the privileged princes of the kingdom. Thereafter, he mentally rehearsed the skill and mastered it.

For using the understanding of mirror neurons for spiritual growth, you can choose your role model on the spiritual path. He or she can be your guru, or guide. Focus on his or her qualities and contemplate on them. Contemplate on his (or her) intentions, his vision, his attitude of service, his devotion, his wisdom, the way he gets into the depth of any topic, the way he spans across multiple topics, his focus, the way he patiently listens, the way he speaks, walks, smiles, his humor, his happiness, his presence of mind, his creativity, his time management, his organization skills, the way he maintains poise in the face of difficulties, his decision making ability, his outlook towards situations, his extraordinary answers to seemingly trivial questions.

By constantly thinking about your spiritual ideal, you feel as if you are walking hand in hand with him or her. By this observation, your mirror neurons will get fired and believe as if you are doing it. Also, when you put yourself into his or her shoes by asking yourself what he or she would have done in certain circumstances, you can merge the actions and mindset of your role model with your own, using the mirror neuron system to optimize your skill and performance in those circumstances.

Thus, in due course of time, you will learn everything about your role model and your mirror neurons will imitate him or her. You will master all those skills not only externally but imbibe the mindset internally as well. Soon you will be able to emulate your spiritual ideal. Walking in his or her footsteps will become a way of life. If you were to acquire all these skills on your own, it would have been a humongous task. Mirror neurons makes the job easy. Thus, whatever you focus on becomes your reality one day.

If you don't have anyone specific to focus on, you can write down the qualities you want. Read biographies of people who had those qualities, watch movies where these qualities are demonstrated. Visualize yourself enacting those qualities. Be in the company of those who possess these qualities.

You need to be always careful about what you observe as your mirror neurons are constantly imitating whatever you observe. Remember by observing virtues in others you are planting seeds for your future. Your mirror neurons will soon make it a reality for you by manifesting these qualities.

When you are in the company of those who uplift you, whose presence calls forth your best, you are putting your mirror neurons into action at that time. The ability to learn from other people's triumphs and mistakes without having to experience them firsthand is a function of the mirror neuron system. Choose the right *Satsang*, the company of spiritual seekers. This will help you in progressing in leaps and bounds on your spiritual path.

10

Be Happy and Attract the Best in Life

Be Free from Negative Bias

Observing the hectic pace at which activities are going on in the world around you, you may wonder why everyone is working so hard. People seem to be working day and night. If you ask a housewife, she would say that she is doing it for the wellbeing of her family. An office goer would say he is doing so to be able to give the best to his family. An entrepreneur would say he wants to utilize his potential to the fullest. A scientist would say that he or she is participating in the creative evolution of the world.

The core intention behind this daily grind is nothing but happiness. And this is not one-time happiness; we want it on a continuous basis. Isn't it really absurd that we need to struggle so hard for happiness? However, in the pursuit of happiness, many of us are unhappy. We are unhappy with our jobs, relationships, money, career, etc.

Research has shown that most people have the tendency to focus on the negative rather than the positive. We tend to see negative in people more than the positive. If we hear a sad song, we can easily relate to it and become sad. Whereas if we listen to a happy song, we don't necessarily feel equally happy. If we become sad, we do our best to get rid of it at the earliest. Whereas when we are happy, we are worried that it won't last forever, so we anticipate the next bout of sorrow bidding its turn. This is known as a negative bias. This happens because negative experiences trigger stronger and memorable emotions than the positive ones.

If you ask someone to narrate the miserable experiences in his life, he would just go on and on with his or her never ending list. He or she may be able to describe even the minutest of details from their memory. However, if you ask them to list some of their memorable happy events, they would fall short. If you ask them to count their blessings, he or she might even become speechless since nothing of significance comes to their mind. Why does this happen?

Right from our childhood, we have observed our surroundings and have borrowed its belief system. We feel that it's natural to feel sad whereas we always reserve our happiness for the future. We have a criterion that only when we acquire something worthwhile, we can be happy. Following are some of the cases when we become happy:

- Score well in the exams
- Satisfy others' expectations
- Get promoted on the job
- Get a favorite gadget
- Watch a favorite movie
- Go out for dinner
- Go on a vacation with family

- Someone pats us on our back

Thus, happiness has become conditional.

Not only that, we have become dependent upon others for our own happiness. It's like our happiness is in their custody, they are holding our remote control in their pockets. If they wish, then only we can be happy. It's so ridiculous that we are taking all the painstaking, relentless efforts to attain our goal and don't become happy. We become happy only when someone approves it and says that it was worthwhile to achieve it.

Further, by indulging in sensual pleasures we expect to derive happiness but they bring only momentary happiness. If we watch a movie today, we get bored watching it again. So, we want variety. The same is applicable with any pleasure associated with taste, smell, sound, and touch. We can eat a pineapple cake for one day, but not every day. We can listen to our favorite song for some time, but can't listen to it for the whole day. The same thing which gives us pleasure ends up being painful when it's done in excess. If you indulge in sensual pleasures for pursuing happiness, then be rest assured that you can never be permanently happy.

 Brain Research

All of the above experiences have wired our brain in such a way that we have become more prone to sorrow than happiness. When people don't behave as per our expectation, when events don't turn out as per our wish, our brain releases chemicals which generates an unhappy feeling. Every unhappy event brings out the memories of similar past unhappy events. Thus, the neural pathway of the new event gets wired together with that of the past events and together they send chemicals to the entire body. Hence, we experience unhappy emotions. As a result, even a small problem appears like a big mountain. Our entire focus shifts to the negative aspects and rarely we focus on the positive side of life. Our mental condition impacts our physical health. We get drained. We go through anxiety, depression and stress.

On the contrary, if we consciously choose to be happy in the face of a so called unhappy event, then we are helping our brain to rewire it in a new way. As most of us have been unconsciously programmed to be unhappy since our childhood, it may take a lot of effort to become happy initially. When you see the results, you will be encouraged to continue. Gradually, with sustained efforts your brain will change itself through neuroplasticity. When we become happy, our brain releases happy hormones. These make us feel good, reduce our anxiety and stress. They make us energetic, positive and productive. If we continue to be happy even during unhappy events, soon our brain will get rewired completely and no incident can make us unhappy. Further, with every incident our brain would pull out the memories of the past happy events and our happiness count would get multiplied.

 Practical Application

There are countless ways that can make you happy, but it's better to find some which can provide more lasting happiness. Here are some suggested ways to rewire your brain from unhappiness to happiness.

1. Whenever you are unhappy, recollect all the positive things that happened in your life since childhood. Be grateful for them. Gratitude is one of the most powerful emotions. There

are several studies that show that gratitude physically changes the brain. The habit of keeping a journal and writing three things you are grateful for has been proven to wire your brain positively.

2. When your mind blows the event out of proportion, tell yourself that this is not as bad as the mind construes it. It is momentary. Accept it as it is. Become happy and identify reasons why the event is your need of the moment. This changes your perspective and you immediately start looking at the whole scenario positively. In order to develop such a perspective, you need to gain the higher knowledge about life which will help you see everything in the light of wisdom.

3. Ask yourself how was your state before this thought of unhappiness arose in your mind. Your entire state changed right after this thought. So, which state would you prefer to have – the state before the thought or after? Simply by choosing to have the state before the thought, you can regain that positive happy feeling.

4. When you indulge in the negative thoughts and become unhappy, your thoughts drain you. At that time, redirect your thoughts in the new direction. Instead of focusing on the negative aspects of people, focus on the positive qualities you would like to imbibe within you. As you continue thinking about them, you give power to those happy thoughts to manifest in your life. For example, you are unhappy that your boss criticizes you. Focus on how you will be an appreciative leader in the future.

5. When you are unhappy, choose a physical activity such as dancing, going for a walk, practicing yoga, pranayama or

doing exercises. Studies have shown that this will generate happy hormones in you.

6. When you are unhappy, repeat the positive self-affirmations which will instill positive feeling within you. The affirmations can be –

- I am the Divine expression of Life. I have understood how important and extraordinary I am.
- I am completely balanced. In every stage of life, I progress ahead with ease and happiness.
- I look at all my experiences with love, I also look at others with bright love.
- I have every right to be happy in life, I am open to receive all the happiness that life offers.
- Everything happening in my life is good and right as per the divine plan.
- I choose to be happy, I choose to accept the way I am.
- I forgive myself with love and understanding, now I am free, I am freedom.
- I am the one who operates my mind. It is easy to bring my mind into a new mould of thinking. I am letting go of my old fixed pattern of thinking.
- I let go of all those thoughts that impede my progress and stop me from being what I want to be. I release all such thoughts.

By repeating these affirmations, you instruct your mind to focus on them. What you focus on, becomes a reality for you.

7. When you are unhappy, force yourself to break out into a smile. Our facial expressions influence our emotional experience. It's called facial feedback hypothesis. Smiling can greatly improve your mood and reduce stress. Even a fake smile gives the same result as a genuine smile. Further smiling is contagious. So when you smile, others smile back at you. Thus, your relationships improve.

8. If you've travelled by train, you would have experienced that it becomes dark when the train passes through a tunnel. What do you do when the train passes through the tunnel? Your attention turns within, as you can't see anything outside in the darkness. You eagerly await the end of the tunnel, where bright daylight appears. You know that it's just a matter of time before you are ushered in the brightness of daylight.

In the same way, whenever situations that cause negative feelings like sorrow, disappointment, anger, or despair occur, remind yourself:

- I am joy that is travelling through this tunnel of sorrow.
- I am peace travelling through this tunnel of anger.
- I am bright faith, travelling through this tunnel of despair.

As you say so with firm conviction, the tunnel becomes short and love, joy, peace prevails in your life.

Spiritual Insight

Just like the nature of water is wetness, our true nature is happiness. Does water need any external medium to acknowledge it about its wetness? No. Then why do we depend upon external sources to make us happy?

Think about your thoughts as seeds you are sowing in the garden of your life. When you are unhappy, you sow the weeds in your life which are going to create trouble in your future. You will spend a lot of time later to remove these weeds as these would have turned into big trees. When you foresee what is going to happen with these kind of thoughts, you will desist from sowing such weeds. Instead, you can choose to sow the positive seeds which will yield happy, bright future for you.

The reason for our tendency to be unhappy is that our true nature of happiness is shrouded by the web of beliefs, patterns and tendencies of our mind. The more we move away from our true nature, the more we become unhappy. In fact, unhappiness is nothing but a call from God to return back to our true nature. Due to lack of spiritual knowledge, we fail to understand it. We fill the void by fulfilling the desires of our mind and thereby fueling it. No matter what amount of desires we fulfil, our mind never gets satisfied. It always gets ready and waits for something new. In fact, seeking happiness in the world by fulfilling desires is like chasing one's own shadow endlessly. Like the shadow, happiness always eludes us. We experience sorrow, conflict and dissatisfaction when we move away from our true nature.

Instead, you need to take the help of spiritual knowledge to come out of this entanglement. You can listen to truth discourses, read books on truth and gain wisdom. Spiritual techniques like meditation, chanting, self-enquiry, contemplation and forgiveness can help you to regain your original nature which is full of happiness.

When you are unhappy because of someone and have developed negative feelings like hatred, jealousy, anger, etc., mentally seek forgiveness from that person and forgive yourself for causing the unhappiness within you. Tell yourself that the main reason for your unhappiness is not the external person but the ignorance within you. Mentally seek forgiveness from God for your ignorance and pray that you wish to be freed from it; let your life be full of love, joy and peace. You can then chant "love-joy-peace" for some time. This will change your state or mental vibration.

You can also practice meditation when you are unhappy. Thus, instead of becoming unhappy with a negative thought, you use it for invoking peace within. This will enhance your power of discernment and you will be able to differentiate between what is right and wrong for your true spiritual growth. You will be able to handle the whims and fancies of your restless mind. Instead of giving in to the directionless thoughts of your mind, you will gain inner strength and focus on your true positive nature. As you continue with your spiritual practice, gradually you will get rid of your preconceived notions, beliefs and tendencies. As a result, your mind becomes steadfast, obedient, unshaken and loving. Such a mind gets ready to easily surrender itself for the expression of the highest desires of Self through your body-mind. You realize that there is no way to happiness; happiness itself is the way.

As you become happy, your entire disposition changes. It's like you have become a powerful magnet which attracts all the best things in the universe. You start seeing everything in the light of happiness. Things which otherwise seemed impossible will now seem possible to you. You start giving due value to everything instead of paying too much of importance. Your level of acceptance, patience and tolerance increases. Instead of blaming situations and people, you accept everyone as they are and allow them to function whole heartedly. You become more receptive for creative ways of solving problems. Your thoughts are steered in the right direction yielding to the desired results. Your productivity, efficiency improves.

As you become happy, your vibrations match with all those people and objects in the world which are positive. They start getting attracted towards you. Positive things get multiplied in your life. Your social relations improve and you have harmony in your relations.

As you continue to remain happy in and through all circumstances, your presence itself becomes instrumental for making others happy. You become the source of happiness. You are inundated with the best health, wealth, prosperity and peace. You become receptive for new ideas required for raising the level of consciousness of the entire world. Thus, by being happy you not only help yourself, but the world around. You become instrumental to uplift the people around you.

11

Symbology

Unravel the Hidden Secrets

We are surrounded by pictures and images. They inform us as to what we should and shouldn't do. When we look at the national flag, patriotic feelings arise. When we look at pictures of animals, birds and plants, we are reminded of a wild life sanctuary. When we look at the idols of God, devotional feelings arise. Business logos convey more than the image. We understand the portfolio of products and services offered by the companies just by looking at the image. All these pictures and images which are symbols, evoke powerful feelings.

A symbol is a sign, shape, object or image which is used to represent quality, idea or meaning of some abstract concept or a thing. Symbols represent something by association, resemblance or convention. While symbol is something material, it represents and conveys something invisible. A symbol generates a feeling within us, which cannot be always put in words easily. Some symbols have mysterious aspects and are loaded with lot of meaning that can be deciphered when you contemplate deeply. Symbols work on our mind, influence our thoughts, without us being aware of the fact. Symbols can create positive feelings of creativity or they may induce fear in us.

 Brain Research

Babies, when they start learning to speak a language, are first introduced to symbols and then words. The same part of their brain gets activated when they are taught using gestures, pictures vis-à-vis words. Their brain begins the tedious and awesome task of unconsciously reshaping or creating their neural pathways for interpreting pictures and words. With repetition, these neural pathways become highways. As grown-ups, they vividly remember these symbols and words. Later on it becomes natural for them to decode these symbols and translate them into words. They become experts in building sentences and expressing their emotions. It happens so fast at the unconscious level that they too don't realize it. Thus, in the process of learning, their new neural pathways get rewired with the existing pathways.

A picture is worth a thousand words and the message conveyed may be very subtle. When we use words to convey the same, every person interprets it based on their own preconceived meanings. However, a picture is most likely interpreted in the same way by everyone.

Memories, ideas, thoughts, photographs are symbols which are stored in our brain. Symbology is a completely different way of learning using symbols. Symbols are used by others to trigger our thoughts, emotions, wants, needs and actions. In fact, our brain already knows the meaning of most of these symbols. When we repeatedly and consistently focus on the symbols by paying attention, they get triggered and activated in our brain. Our brain creates new neural pathways for all the symbols and their associated meaning and feeling. This includes symbols which our brain already understands and some it doesn't. We deeply feel what the symbols want to convey. If we repeatedly focus on those symbols, those neural pathways become highways. Later just by looking at the symbols, it evokes the feeling along with its meaning.

 Practical Application

Symbology is the process of decoding images, placing them in proper historic context, by finding their origins. Let's understand how the symbols are practically used.

1. Before writing was invented, ancient civilizations passed on information orally in stories and mythologies, accompanied by visual symbols. Certain drawings or pictures were commonly used to denote specific objects or things; thus symbols were born. Mythological stories were written in symbols millennia back. Through the years, civilizations have used symbols to mean many different things. They have become an easy way to point out an ideology, to express an abstract thought or even to denote a group or community who share the same goals. Though meaning of certain symbols varies from place to place, there is a universal agreement over some symbols.

2. Symbols have impacted human culture, art, history, literature, mythology, magic, religion, psychology and even dreams. They span across multiple domains such as magic and mystery, deities and rituals, the animal and plant kingdom,

landscape and the elements, food and Mathematics. Symbols are used in chakras, the tarot and the zodiac, mythical beasts and magical numbers, currencies and emoticons. In fact, if you look around, you will see that you are surrounded by a variety of symbols everywhere. You may not be consciously aware that they are called symbols.

3. Symbols have been used for creating a sentiment, a public mindset, rallying people for a common altruistic cause. Some symbols are controlled and censored in countries where they believe they might fuel rebellion. Thus, symbols have been used for constructive as well as destructive purpose. Organizations like Red Cross have used symbols for raising funds and support for the needy. Literature, art uses symbols to convey deeper and subtler meaning.

4. Symbolism is a nonverbal, nonliterary, visual language, which is passed on from generation to generation. This compelling language contains records of our ancestor's knowledge, historical information, and information about cultural traditions, religions, and customs.

5. Symbols are used in art, literature, and dreams. Interpretation of what it means is to be passed on from one generation to the other. Otherwise the meaning gets lost with the passage of time.

6. Symbols have been used in broadening our understanding of astronomy and astrology. With the help of symbolism, it has been found easy to explain why planets revolve around the Sun, why stars formed constellations. They have helped explore the new dimensions of astronomy.

7. Cosmic symbolism is more related to the impact of cosmos, stars on human life. Hence, it is closely bound with religion.

- The sun is a symbol of cosmic power, the source of energy. The moon is a symbol related with the tide of water. Its luminous presence in the night made it symbolic of hope and enlightenment.

- Moon's constantly evolving form has been given spiritual significance of birth and death. In addition to impacting tides, weather and life, moon is symbolized as a ruler of human destiny. People worship moon on full moon day to get blessings and avoid its curse.

- Sky and everything in it, the moon and stars, thunder and lightning every aspect has a spiritual significance.

- Even mountains have been considered to have divine significance because of their proximity to heaven. Therefore, in mythology gods and goddesses are considered to reside on mountains. It varies as per culture and religion.

- Rivers indicate constant movement and when it joins the ocean it signifies peace. Water itself is a symbol of purity.

🪷 Spiritual Insight

Let's understand how symbology impacts spirituality.

1. Symbology and Idols

Symbols provide the mechanism to access the deeper secrets hidden in our mind. Since ancient times, Self-realized sages have encoded the knowledge of truth in symbolic form in idols. The custom of worshipping idols was passed on from generation to generation. The intention behind the custom was to encourage people to contemplate upon these idols to reveal those secrets.

When one contemplates upon the essential nature of truth and its qualities, the significance of different parts of the idol, one experiences the same truth in the idol. The idol then becomes God in a true sense, rather than a mere statue. If they start seeing God in one idol, the possibility of seeing God in all beings increases. Rarely they understand that they are experiencing the same truth within themselves and those divine qualities are getting activated within them. This contemplation helps them to become instrumental for the expression of the Self through their body-mind. Only when this happens it can be said that the idol has been truly worshipped. Thereby, the true purpose of creating idols is fulfilled. Otherwise, they merely follow the ritual without understanding the actual purpose behind it. When they realize the same truth as the realized sages, they pass it on to the masses so that everyone benefits from their realization.

The idols were created to personify the abstract principles of natural law and vital forces of the nature. The *Shiv-linga* has been conceived by Self-realized sages to represent the original state of Self-in-rest when the world was not manifested. It is the state of nothingness which has also been known as *Shunya-murti*. The Nataraja dance of lord Shiva symbolizes the coming into action of the Self, leading to manifestation of the world. The cycle of creation, maintenance and destruction is being perpetuated in the universe. This has been symbolized by the trinity of Brahma, Vishnu and Mahesh. Thus, different idols symbolize different aspects of God.

2. Symbology and Festivals

Self-realized sages also conceived festivals dedicated to certain Gods. These festivals represent opportunities to worship the qualities represented by the deity. For example, the festival of Navaratri symbolizes the veneration of Shakti which represents the victory over the nine vices of the human mind.

3. Symbology and Remembrance of the Truth

In addition to idols, self-realized sages have also transferred the knowledge of truth in the form of analogies, pictures, poems and hymns. Words are easily forgotten whereas analogies, pictures and poems are easily remembered and can be passed on from one generation to the other. Whoever contemplates on them interprets the hidden meaning behind them and gets to know the deeper truths.

As one becomes an expert in decoding the symbols, gradually he can decode symbols around and open himself to the rich heritage offered by them. He can interpret the deepest truths encoded within them which will lead him to his ultimate path of development.

For a spiritual seeker, a world filled with symbols is infinitely rich and rewarding. It leads him to a greater understanding of his true nature, bringing a fresh perspective about life. Symbols in everyday life can become reminders of truth. A simple thing like a ladder can be a reminder of spiritual progress. Looking at a white lotus rising from the mud one can be reminded of the highest spiritual understanding. He can learn to function in the world while being detached from the world and express his fullest potential. The lotus has a choice of being dirty as the mud or become separate from the mud. When it chooses to become separate, the highest expression is put forth by it. The white lotus represents purity.

Thus, if a spiritual seeker associates truth with everything he sees around, the same thing which used to delude him in the external illusory world will start reminding him of his inner true Self. Instead of getting entangled in the world outside, he will focus within. Later on just by looking at the symbols he will be reminded of the truth. Thus, the symbols will help him constantly remain in the bliss of truth. For that matter, no symbol is useless, as each and every symbol has a purpose.

4. Symbology and Religion

Symbols were important in early societies as they helped people to live in a more harmonious way and also to understand and strive towards their divine enlightenment. Symbols were used to identify communities, groups of people. Religious symbols greatly helped in this endeavor. Religious symbols are iconic representations of specific religions or specific concepts within those religions. Following are some religious symbols:

Wheel of Dharma represents Buddhism. It symbolizes Gautama Buddha's teachings on the path to Nirvana.

The syllable "om" or "Aum" represents Hinduism. The vibration of "Aum" symbolizes the manifestation of God in form. Before creation began, it was emptiness or void. "Aum" is the reflection of the absolute reality which has no beginning or the end, which embraces all that exists. It represents the creation, maintenance and destruction aspects of the divine energy which controls the universe. "Aum" is also chanted as a mantra in the name of God, the vibration of the Supreme.

The Christian cross has traditionally been a symbol representing Christianity.

The star and crescent symbol represents Islam religion.

The symbol of Khanda represents Sikhism.

5. Symbology and Qualities

While treading on the spiritual path, you may want to get rid of certain tendencies and habits which are slowing you down. At such times, you can take the help of symbols. For example, if you want to improve your concentration, you may choose the symbol of a magnifying lens. Lens symbolizes convergence of light rays into a single focal point. You may also use the symbol of a burning candle and constantly focus on the flame.

If you want to get rid of fear and build courage, you may choose the symbol of a ship navigating in water. Ship symbolizes courage. The way the ship sails in water against all odds like storms and still reaches its destination, you too can sail through this journey of life and attain your goal.

Thus, you can choose different symbols for every unwanted habits or tendencies you want to get rid of and new habits or qualities you want to inculcate. Consistently focus on these external symbols. Tell your brain the purpose and goal behind it. Your brain will then start creating new neural pathways related to these symbols, their associated purpose and goal inside your brain. The more you focus on these symbols, the stronger these neural pathways will become. It's not that the old habits will not come in your way. They will pull you back into your comfort zone intermittently. Still by using the symbols you can steadily progress towards your goal.

When your focus is on courage, you will notice incidents that will create fear and uncomfortable feeling within you. You may even feel it is almost impossible to move ahead in your journey. Still you need to consciously focus on the symbol, in this case the ship, and remind yourself that you are in favor of courage, not fear. Fear has come as an outcome of the old neural pathway. If you act out of fear, then you are strengthening the old neural pathway. Whereas if you take action imbibing courage, then you are helping to build the new neural pathway and eliminate fear forever.

Same is the case when you focus on concentration. You will notice situations that will pull you in multiple directions, away from your goal. At that time, you need to be alert and aware and remind yourself that you are in favor of single pointed focus, not distraction. This will help you channel your energies in that direction. Keep yourself focused on the symbol you have selected, which is magnifying lens or the burning candle.

As you consistently focus on the symbols, you help your brain create robust pathways. Gradually, new pathways will become highways and the old pathways will wear off. Thereafter, whenever you look at these symbols, your brain will interpret the hidden meaning behind them. New neural pathways will get activated and new habits and qualities will get inculcated within you. You will get the confidence that nothing is impossible.

6. Symbology and the Hidden Treasure Chest

With the help of symbology, in addition to creating new neural pathways, you can also unearth certain hidden neural pathways which are already there in your brain but were rarely used. Some of these neural pathways are related with spiritual techniques such as

- Chanting
- Doing penance
- The path of karma
- The path of devotion
- The path of wisdom
- The path of meditation
- The path of absolute knowledge

If you associate them with certain symbols and train your brain about the purpose and goal behind it, your brain will activate these existing hidden neural pathways for your service.

Thus, as you start utilizing symbology to its fullest, neural highways are created and the symbols start working for you. The blue print of your brain will change to such an extent that just by looking at the external symbols, you will be reminded of the internal neural pathways. Your life will be full of love, joy and peace. You will rapidly progress in your spiritual journey.

12

Love

Revel in the Bliss of Your True Nature

Love could be between a couple, between parents and children, between siblings. It could be between a master and his disciple. It could be between a devotee and God. It could be for the country viz. patriotism. It could be for animals or concepts (someone may be in love with his or her vision) or non-living things too.

Many a times, things which otherwise seem impossible become possible only in love. A pregnant lady bears all her pain in love for her baby. There is power in love. You may have heard examples where a mother stopped a heavy vehicle with her bare hands since her son could have come under the vehicle.

Love has been praised by poets, writers since ancient times. It has been one of the main topics on which most of the literature is written. The core theme of most of the movies and plays is also love.

Sages and saints have sung hymns and devotional songs (*bhajan*) being in love with God. Their devotion helped them transcend their limitations and experience oneness with God.

You may wonder why love has been regarded so highly. What exactly is the power of love and why does one become ready to even sacrifice one's own life and self-interest in love for someone else? Let's understand what happens in the brain when it comes to love.

 **Brain Research**

Research has shown that when individuals see or think about those whom they love, their brain generates chemicals which gives them a good feeling. Their reward circuits get activated. Feelings of pleasure, expectation, focused attention and motivation arise in them. They get a boost of energy to transcend their limitations and achieve things which otherwise would have been impossible to achieve.

You may have heard the saying "Love is blind." Let's understand the neural basis behind this. In addition to the positive feelings love brings, it also deactivates the neural pathway responsible for negative emotions, such as fear and social judgment. These positive and negative feelings involve two neural pathways. When one feels love for the other person, the neural machinery responsible for making critical assessments of the person they love shuts down. Hence, they fail to see any shortcomings in the person they love.

When someone falls in love, the chemicals generated in their brain produce a variety of physical and emotional responses. To start with, level of the stress hormone cortisol increases in the brain. This is what is experienced as a racing heart, sweaty palms, flushed cheeks, feelings of passion and anxiety, etc.

Being love-struck also releases high levels of dopamine, a chemical that gets the reward system going. Dopamine activates the reward circuit, helping to make love a pleasurable experience.

As love progresses, oxytocin, also known as the love hormone, increases. This is what provokes feelings of contentment, calmness and security.

When one becomes an addict to a substance, he or she needs to increase their dose in order to get the same kick that they used to get earlier. Research shows that the pleasurable experience one gets in love is similar to the euphoria associated with the use of drugs or alcohol. In other words, it's like addiction. When one doesn't get sustained pleasurable feeling in relationship, they feel rejected, depressed and lonely. They feel the other person is the cause of their sorrow and if that person continues to love them as per their beliefs and expectations, then alone they can be happy. Thus, they completely depend upon the external environment to sustain the pleasurable feeling within them.

If the other person fails to behave as per their expectations, their negative neural pathway of love, also called as hatred, forces them to find loopholes in their relationship. When this happens, some people still continue with their relationship without love and put the harmony in their relationship at stake. Some people try to reconcile their relationship through mutual discussion and arrive at some common agreement to proceed with the same relationship further. Some people take help of addictions to seek relief. There are others who just can't continue with their relationship and choose to separate. Later on they may get into another relationship. Little do they know that they are doing it just to satisfy their reward center to get the same pleasurable feeling.

Having seen what happens with love in our brains, let us look at the practical application.

 Practical Application

Once you understand what happens in the brain, the idea is to make sure that oxytocin levels increase, cortisol does not increase and there is no addiction to dopamine.

First let us look at not being addicted to personalized love from an individual. Access the feeling of love within you. Be loving to others. But do not try to get love only from one or two people. Every person has his own mental definition of love. He feels and acts as if his interpretation of love is the universal truth. He uses himself as a yardstick and tends to project his own emotional state onto others while assessing the world around him. However, his emotional state can distort his understanding of others' emotions, in particular if these emotions are completely different than his own. If his interpretation of love doesn't match with that of others, it may prove to be a criticism or a punishment for the other person.

The question then arises how not to be dependent only on a few people for love. How should one get increased levels of oxytocin in the brain without increased levels of cortisol or dependency on dopamine? The answer lies in compassion. The more compassionate you are towards others, all the good benefits of love (increased levels of oxytocin) can be experienced. It also reduces dependency on love from a handful of people.

Compassion means showing empathy, sympathy, care, concern, sensitivity to others. It is showing up more honestly, being more present, free from any physical and mental distractions, remaining open to feedback and really listening. It is kindness, caring and willingness to help others. When we are not compassionate, we show indifference, cruelty and harsh criticism.

We may find it hard to be compassionate all the time. But we can develop more compassion through training. With this, our brain's neural circuitry can be rewired. As you train yourself to be compassionate, gradually you will have stronger, happy and healthier relationships. You will feel more confident and mentally stable, maintain a healthier lifestyle and bounce back from adversity more effectively.

Following are few of the several ways research suggests that can improve our compassion:

1. Meditation: Practice meditations that focus on qualities like forgiveness, love and kindness. It will help you witness emotional reaction to the suffering of yourself and others' in turn. This will increase both compassion towards others in need, and also self-compassion.

   Everyday spend some time to practice forgiveness. Mentally seek forgiveness from those whom you hurt, knowingly or unknowingly, through your feelings, thoughts, speech or action. Also, forgive those who hurt you, knowingly or unknowingly, through their feelings, thoughts, speech or action. Express love towards them and thank them for being in your life.

   Forgiveness is incomplete till such time that you haven't forgiven yourself. To be loving and grateful to everything and everyone, first be loving and grateful to yourself. Love yourself and pardon yourself of any mistakes committed by you. Free yourself of any grudges hold on till now. Once you fill yourself with love and gratitude, you can serve others from a place of overflowing love, energy, and abundance. Your presence can uplift them.

Besides practicing forgiveness as a part of your meditation, practice loving-kindness too. It's a practice to choose happiness not only for your own betterment or progress but for the wellbeing of the entire mankind. It is about uplifting others in such a manner that together we can have a more harmonious, stable and loving surrounding. This journey begins with you. In your own individual capacity, you hold the power to heal and spread good vibes by giving mental and spiritual positivity. You remind yourself that you deserve peace and happiness and extend the same for your family, friends, neighbors, and everyone else in the world. In an unforced way, send compassionate wishes, loving thoughts, blessings for the wellbeing of anyone you remember, no matter where they are.

For example, suppose you see a speeding motorist driving rashly on the road. Instead of thinking of all the possible accidents that could occur to him due to his rash driving, you will wish for a safe journey for him instead of scorning him. You will pray to God to take care of him. If you see an ambulance passing by on the road, you will send your healing vibrations to the patient and wish him good health.

As you practice this daily, you will find your heart has begun to fill with love, kindness, benevolence and friendliness. You will feel oneness and compassion for everyone you see or imagine.

2. Practice Gratitude: Gratitude plays an important role in everyone's life. Whatever we are grateful for, those things multiply in our life. Appreciate the qualities that everyone has including you. Be grateful for your strengths, accomplishments, opportunities you have received, people around you, support from the environment, your relationships, the way you have been guided in the journey of your life. The more you focus on them, it makes it easier to cope with harder times and weaknesses. When you appreciate the qualities in people, you ignore their weaknesses. You become more compassionate about them instead of getting into criticism or judgment. It helps build a harmonious platform with people.

However, this is still a personalized love. Though apparently selfless, it is rooted in desires and satisfactions. Let us look at deeper insights than just compassion.

Spiritual Insight

We have been brought up in a society that judges love based on conditions. Almost all of us have been raised in a belief-system of conditional love. We have been taught that love is something to be earned. We have been made to believe that we can receive love only when we fit into expectations of people. If we are not good enough, we will be deprived of love. If someone does not love us back, they don't deserve our love. Hence, we have been manipulating love based on these beliefs.

These beliefs have influenced the collective psyche of families, groups, communities, societies since generations to such an extent that love has been reduced to fear of denial. While love is the all-pervasive essence of everything, the false notions of love have caused fear to be perpetuated into all areas of our lives.

Most people today live a superficial life; they live at the surface of the ocean of love. If you see what's going on in the Facebook accounts of people, you will realize that they are merely "Surface-book" accounts. People wish to make themselves known to others only on the surface level. But how will they make themselves known to others when they don't know themselves? Have they ever taken a dip below the surface? Do they know the vastness of the ocean of their true being? Those who dove deep into the ocean will tell you how blissful and peaceful their reality is.

What lies beneath the surface is – oneness; oneness of all creations of the Lord. The same consciousness resides in each one of us. The same energy expresses itself through each one of us. On the outside we may all look different but the truth is that we all exist in the same inner experience. True love means awareness of this oneness. This "oneness" is our Self; the universal Self, the real "I". It is the same life principle that pervades everyone and everything. It is the reason we are alive.

We have all experienced this oneness at some point or the other. We have all experienced it as infants. As infants we were literally swimming deep in the ocean of true love. But now we have risen to the surface. Our purpose now is to re-enter the ocean and stabilize in it.

It is now time that we, as a society, shift from the paradigm of false conditional love into the essence of pure unconditional love. We need to let go of so many beliefs to be in the essence of pure love.

We need to understand that we are the source of love and true love can be experienced only through giving, not through seeking. Howsoever hard you try to seek it outside, you can never find true and everlasting love in the external world. You will keep yearning for appreciation, for consideration, for approval from people, due to this fallacy.

By knowing that you are the source of love, you can love yourself. Instead of waiting to receive love from the world, ask yourself, "Why do I need an agent to love myself?" Waiting for the world to love you, is like hiring an agent to love yourself! If you receive love, it is merely a bonus. In fact, people who exist in our life are not here to love us. They are here to remind us that we are the source of love.

When you entertain negative emotions like fear and guilt, you dishonor your true nature of love. It is time for you to honor yourself as the source of love. You have undertaken this human journey to realize and express the boundless love that you truly are. It is time to embrace love as your true nature.

A truth seeker can attain his final goal only when his ego surrenders in devout love of God. He transcends all limitations to be in love of God. He experiences the bliss of pure love and becomes an epitome of love himself. His presence is one of unconditional love for all beings. He feels oneness with everyone and accepts them as they are. He sees the world as a beautiful and faultless expression of the creator. That is why it is said, in true love one doesn't fall in love, one rises in love. Increase the quality of devotion in your life to rise in love.

13

Freedom from Exaggeration

See Things As They Are

Sometimes we stumble upon situations where we exaggerate them or blow them out of proportion. At such times, because of our distorted perception, the situation appears to be worse than it actually is. Let's understand this more through a few scenarios.

1. Anusha wants to learn swimming but the moment she enters the pool she feels that she will drown. So, she gives up swimming altogether. On the other hand, Anita doesn't have any such fear. So, she learns swimming in a short time and even becomes an ace champion.

2. Whenever Asha sneezes, she immediately begins to worry that she will catch a cold that will lead to a bout of bad bronchitis. Soon, she sees her fears turning out to be true.

3. When Reema visits her brother, he continues with his chore and doesn't pay heed to her. She considers it as a humiliating behavior and keeps brooding over the situation, thinking not to visit him ever again.

4. Vineet and Kiran have to collaborate on a project. However, they had some conflict in the past. Hence, both are hesitant to speak to each other. Even if they strike a conversation, it leads to arguments.

5. When Nisha sees a lizard, she gets into frenzy to get rid of it by all means.

Now, let's understand what the brain research has to say about all this.

 Brain Research

Whatever we look at creates an inverted image on our retina. Our eyes collect all the visual data and pass it on to the visual centre in our brain. The visual centre then reinverts the image, interprets the visual information into what we can understand. The interpretation of the image differs from person to person as each one has different set of data related to it. The data could be in terms of information of the object such as color, shape and depth of the object, emotions associated with it, or any past data processed for similar visuals. Accordingly, those neurons fire together and wire together making the experience more intense. Each person then looks at the image with the distorted perception created by their respective interpretations and determines their action accordingly. This filtered perception doesn't allow them to see the image as it is. Instead, it adds an extra emotional charge into it. This tendency of the brain to make a mountain out of a molehill is called magnification, exaggeration or "zoom pattern".

The exaggeration pattern works even when we go through situations in life. At such times, our thoughts and beliefs play an important role in forming these distorted perceptions. All the associated neurons pertaining to the past experiences fire together and we experience an emotional charge while facing the current event. Most of the times, as we are unaware of these intricacies, our perverted view of the situation forces our mechanical programming to take charge of our response. Thus, we see ourselves giving the same old response, leaving us no scope to experience the event afresh. If we have brooded over a similar event in the past, we will repeat the same even in the present as well. If we have become angry in a similar event in the past, we may become angry even in the present. It's akin to a machine producing the same output again and again.

As a matter of fact, the new situation could be different than the old one. However, if we are not alert and aware, then our brain immediately associates the event with its past memory and makes it a veritable hell. It magnifies the event to such an extent that all the other aspects including both positives as well as negatives around the event get filtered out. Our vision of reality becomes darkened and distorted. We believe the situation to be far worse than it actually is. Thus it can be said that whatever sufferings we go through are not because of the external situations and people, but because of our brain's interpretation of the event and the context. Whenever such events recur, the associated neurons fire together giving us the same painful experience. The brain's recording plays so fast that these thoughts occur automatically and we find it impossible to transcend them.

One may wonder if everything happens automatically then is it possible to give a new response? Research suggests that it is possible. Using neuro linguistic programming (NLP), we can dis-associate from these past programming and associate a new programming with the event, thereby altering our experience of the event.

It's a common observation that we are better off at solving others' problems than our own. We personalize our problems and get stuck in them. When we look at others' problems, we watch them from a distance as an observer without adding any colors to it. Hence, we think better. We can extend this technique further and use it for dis-associating from our own past experiences.

 Practical Application

Let's look at its practical application now. We will practice a technique here with which you can easily dis-associate from your past programming. First read the instructions, understand them clearly and then practice them.

a. Close your eyes.

b. Think of any event from the past, remembering which you feel very sad. Avoid seeing something very traumatic. It could be an event where someone scolded you, or you lost something.

c. Play this event on the screen of your mind with all the colors added to it. Hear the sounds in the scene – they can be surrounding sounds, words spoken by people involved in the scene including you. Smell the scene, watch the expressions of all the people in the scene. Now notice how you feel in that scene, what thoughts are running in your mind.

d. Now remove colors from the scene and see it in black and white colors. Watch the event from a distance by visualizing it being played on a screen. It's as if you are sitting in the projection booth and seeing the screen. You are no longer into the scene. Play the event on this screen from start to end. Hear the people involved in the scene speaking in the voice of cartoon characters like Mickey Mouse and Donald Duck instead of their own voice. See the scene in a fast motion. Now, make the animated video into a still picture like a drawing. Disintegrate it into infinite number of small dots and imagine the entire scene and the screen being dissolved into the universe.

e. Now, slowly open your eyes. Take 2-3 deep breaths and close your eyes again. Try to recall the same event and watch your feelings. Do you feel grieved even now? You will wonder that the feeling of grief is no longer there.

You can use this technique to re-record any of your past experiences of grief, even as old as the time when you were a child. Those events were recorded with your understanding at that time. Now, you can dis-associate them from the past recording and associate a new recording as per your revised understanding with it.

As you disintegrate the event and dissolve it into the universe, the impression of the event on your subconscious mind subsides. You have become free from the event and the associated negative emotions. Hence, when you try to recall the event, it doesn't make you as sad. This helps you see every event afresh without the interference of the exaggeration pattern of the brain.

When we face any incident, our brain first gathers the sensory inputs. It feels and smells the environment around, hears the surrounding voices, watches the expressions of the people around.

It then scans the memory for any such past events. If it gets any, it associates it with the present event and views the event using the filter of the perceptions created in the past. Let's understand it with the above examples.

1. When Anusha was small, once she fell in a pool of water. Thereafter she was always afraid of entering into water. She fears that she might drown. Although she has now grown up, still this thought overpowers her and her body trembles with fear. The same emotions and bodily sensations replay in her body-mind and she gives up swimming. On the other hand, Anita doesn't have any such past memory, so she learns swimming smoothly and effortlessly.

   Using the above technique, Anusha can play the entire recording on an imaginary screen of what exactly happened with her when she enters into water. As she sees the memory in black and white disassociate from it and disintegrates the still picture into infinite tiny dots, she can erase her fear of getting drowned. She can now learn swimming too.

2. Reema has felt humiliated. Her thought forces her to have a partial view of the situation and makes her unhappy. Reema can now play the recording of the entire incident on a screen. She can see her brother speaking like the cartoon character, Mickey Mouse. She can even see Mickey's red nose. The entire scene becomes one of comedy for her. She can minimize the impact of the event in her mind. When she recalls the incident again, she is no longer unhappy with it. Instead in the scene, she is calm, composed and even a bit amused.

3. Because of her past fearful memory, Nisha sees a tiny lizard to be as big as a dinosaur. Hence, the sight of the lizard forces her to mechanically repeat her past actions. The fact is that instead of panicking, she can perform the same action peacefully.

When Nisha plays the entire scene of how she is afraid of the lizard in her mind, she witnesses her fear coming from the past. But now, she can see her character as a giant and the lizard as a tiny speck. If she can see the scene in black and white and projected on a screen while she is in the safety of the projection booth, she may even laugh at it. As the entire scene is disintegrated into tiny dots and dissolved in the universe, the scene no longer can have a hold on her. When she recalls it, she sees it afresh with a calm and cool mind.

Such guided imagery techniques have helped in reducing postoperative discomfort as well as chronic pain related to cancer, arthritis, and physical injury. Further, it has helped in overcoming phobias and facing the challenges afresh. This can be used for managing the stress of public performance among musicians, enhancing athletic and competitive sports ability, and training medical students in surgical skills. People who have been rejected in interviews can use this technique to succeed in their forthcoming interviews. For that matter, this technique can be used for any past memory which you don't want and wish to change it for better or completely discard it. Once the image is cleared or changed at the mental level, it reflects on the physical plane automatically.

🪷 Spiritual Insight

It is only when we are in the present that we can unleash our latent potential and explore our infinite possibilities. However, living in the present becomes difficult as whatever we see, hear, smell, touch, or taste are associated with our past impressions. Our mind has created packets of those experiences and stored them in memory. Whenever we go through similar experiences, our mind first opens these packets and tries to judge the experience based on them. As a result, we rarely experience anything afresh. We continue with our age-old opinions about people. We hardly question our opinions and never consider that people may have changed by now.

The exaggeration pattern reflects in most aspects of our life. At a physical level, because of this pattern our mind announces the pain to be more severe than what it actually is. At the mental level, this pattern forces us to indulge in deceit by exaggerating certain facts and giving a perverted view of the situation. At the social level, because of this pattern we may have a distorted view of relationships. Based on the valuation of our mind, we may favor or discard certain relations. At the financial level, this pattern will overstate certain things which are not at all in line with our goal. If we are not alert, we may fall for it and make wrong decisions.

The solution lies at the spiritual level. Instead of using guided imagery, you may just meditatively witness the event all over again without getting entangled into it. If you find witnessing it in your mind difficult, you may resort to the guided imagery of seeing it projected on a screen. Witnessing any event dispassionately and seeing things as they are, is one of the most powerful spiritual practices. Such witnessing automatically leads to healing of past memories.

14

Freedom from Gadgets

Gadgets are the New Cigarettes

A young patient contacts a doctor to treat his pain. The doctor asks him, "Do you exercise regularly?" The patient replies, "Of course, I do." The doctor asks him, "What kind of exercises?" The young chap enthusiastically says, "I play lot of cricket, football and tennis." The doctor is very happy. He asks him, "And how long do you play?" The patient shrugs and replies, "Until my mobile gets discharged."

Humor apart, it shows how most of us have become addicted to excessive use of handheld devices such as mobile phones and tablets. Instead of playing outdoor real world games or actually connecting with people socially, we are glued to the virtual world through screen based gadgets.

In a recent study conducted on the total time spent on mobile apps, it is found that the most active smartphone users in India spend more than 4 hours every day—the equivalent of half a standard workday—on mobile apps. More than 150 million people use social media to keep in touch with friends, share photographs and videos and post regular updates of their movements and thoughts. Indians, on an average, spend 28 hours on mobile, 4 hours on TV and 2 hours on print every week.

In a research conducted on 1319 people in the age group of 16 to 51 years, with a mean age of 21.24, it was found that 1.4% of the total were internet addicts. Out of them, some were detected with depressive tendencies due to excessive use of internet. It was discovered that addicts spent proportionately more time browsing sexually gratifying websites, online gaming sites and online communities.

 Brain Research

We have an inherent tendency to see things around us and respond accordingly. This way, we become aware of any unpredictable events in our surroundings. Our brains are programmed to see ear-to-ear. Information coming from the eyes is interpreted and turned into action by our brain. However, when we are glued to the screen right in front of our nose continually for long hours, besides harming our eyes, this also brings about negative changes in our brain. Our field of view narrows to a smaller box-like zone right in front of our eyes. Our brain learns to categorize everything outside of this box as a distraction unworthy of attention and gets good at filtering out anything not right in front of us. By developing sustained attention in the central view, our peripheral vision suffers, and our view of the world slowly contracts. Peripheral vision has been associated with awareness, calmness, relaxation, etc. Its opposite – foveal vision – which is a focused vision on an object in front of us has been associated with stress, faster heartbeats, fight or flight mode, etc.

Interacting with screens shifts the nervous system into fight-or-flight mode which leads to dysregulation and disorganization of various biological systems. As a result, one becomes increasingly unable to modulate one's mood and attention. One may respond differently when he is playing a video game vis-à-vis sending a text message. Thus, their self-regulation and stress management becomes less efficient.

Our brains and lives are invigorated and nourished by paying attention and being mindful. Our field of view decreases with age. Over time, we become immune to noticing visual changes around us and our eyes move less often. However, as we continue to be glued to screens for a longer time, we in turn self-induce these neurological changes in our brains well in advance than the anticipated biological changes. As a result, our brains and bodies get conditioned not to pay attention and not to react to the unexpected. Our brain considers almost everything as uninteresting and unimportant, which makes for a flat, dull existence. Thus, by living in a smaller visual box, we in turn train our brain to dim the very spark of life and brightness of our spirit.

Because of too much indulgence in screens, many youngsters lack the ability to communicate or concentrate away from their screens. Their social relations are at stake. They lack in face to face communication and are unable to understand emotional context. As a result, their social interactions have become more awkward, and there is greater misinterpretation during face-to-face meetings.

Exposure to blue light and electromagnetic waves from screens in the evening and late night causes suppression of melatonin levels in the brain. Melatonin regulates our sleep-wake cycles. Low levels of melatonin cause sleep deficiency and changes alertness. Chronic suppression of melatonin has been associated with increased risk of certain cancers. Thus, it is very important to ensure that one does not go to sleep viewing a screen.

Technology has touched deep aspects of the lives of people in such a way that they prefer to use technology than their own brains. This has led to lowered development of cognitive skills of their brains. Social media sites are said to shorten attention spans, encourage instant gratification and make people more self-centered. Research suggests that this over-engaging in websites that serve to replace normal social interactions might be linked with psychological disorders like depression and addiction.

Input of multiple technologies is leading to the inability to stick with any one thought for longer than a few seconds. People's ability to focus on long detailed content has shrunk. Creativity and imagination are also lost in this constant use of technology.

During the toddler years, the brain triples in size and continues to develop until adult years. Studies have shown that too much exposure to screen-based gadgets may negatively affect a child's brain functioning, and may even cause attention deficit, cognitive delays, impaired learning, increased impulsivity, and decreased ability for self-regulation. Excessive gadget usage and online activity for toddlers can result in depression and bipolar disorder as they mature. Toddlers react with tantrums and uncontrollable behavior when their devices are taken away. Their withdrawal symptoms are observed to be similar to that of alcoholics or heroin addicts.

Continuous focus on what content is available next on our gadgets excites our neurons and releases the neurotransmitter dopamine into our brain's pleasure centers. This in turn causes the experience to be perceived as pleasurable. This state of mind places the brain in constant crisis as it is continually on the alert for new information that will bring on the next dose of dopamine.

Some people become obsessed with these pleasure-seeking experiences and engage in compulsive behavior such as a need to keep playing a screen game, constantly check email or social media, or compulsively watch brain numbing videos. At times, this addiction becomes more harmful than even cigarette smoking, resulting into Internet Use Disorder (IUD). People with IUD have a preoccupation with the Internet, withdrawal symptoms when the substance (Internet) is no longer available, loss of other interests, and unsuccessful attempts to quit. Research shows that internet addiction is associated with structural and functional changes in the brain regions involving emotional processing, executive attention, decision making and cognitive control.

 Practical Application

Although gadgets have lot of positive aspects, their improper use leads to negative consequences. Hence, in order to regulate their usage and put them to their best use, you may want to bear the following considerations for their usage.

    a.   It is found that spatial experience actually changes brain structures. Hence, it is preferable to spend some time in the natural world. Go in open air, take a walk, play real world games. You can take it as a break during your work hours.

b. Instead of completely relying on gadgets for communication, have face to face communication wherever possible, whenever time permits.

c. Wherever possible, try to make use of your brain instead of using gadgets. If you are going somewhere, instead of using GPS, try to use physical maps. It will help your brain develop spatial faculties internally. Try doing calculations in your brain than immediately using the calculator. You may at minimum estimate a range as the mathematical answer using your head and use the calculator to see how much you have varied from your estimate.

d. It is found that children are now learning how to use gadgets first even before they could walk or even tie their shoelaces. Hence, instead of giving in to their whims, parents should restrict their exposure to gadgets. They should decide their children's time on gadgets. Instead of allowing them to play TV or other gadgets, they should sing, read or talk to their children. Encourage them to play in open air. Encourage face to face communication than through gadgets.

e. Find some engaging projects that require the five senses, hand/brain coordination, solo or group activity.

f. Plan your schedule in such a way that you will have breaks in between which will allow you to be away from your screens. Avoid binge watching television serials or unwanted entertainment on your gadgets. It is found that people have met with accidents because of frequent checking of emails or messages, updates on social media. Hence, it is important to arrive at a schedule of fixed intervals when you will check your gadgets. Once a month, go on a gadget free diet for a full day or half a day. Live without gadgets for a day to begin reducing your dependence on them.

g. As mobile phones are mini radiation centers, do not constantly keep them close to your body (on your body). Try to keep them away as far as possible. If it's possible either switch them off at night (or put them on airplane mode) or put them in another room. Use them only when it's really required.

h. The kind of messages which are exchanged through social networking can be highly stressful and even intimidating to our emotional wellbeing. People are compelled to adhere to pseudo-social norms on social networking platforms. This strengthens their dependency on social approval for their emotional wellbeing. Try to minimize their use as much as possible.

Just because everyone around you seem to be mired in gadgets, do not fall for this herd tendency. Chart your life path free from gadgets to the extent possible using them productively.

Spiritual Insight

Dependency on gadgets gives rise to habits that hamper our spiritual growth. Our mind constantly gets into the tendency of selecting a sensational topic, chasing after it and is distracted from the present moment. We believe that constantly being updated is making us intelligent or more communicative. However, they make our minds dull and desensitized and put our sensory organs under stress to always hanker after something to be happy. Thus, our mind is always in flight, follow or "find out" mode instead of remaining in the present. No amount of indulgence satisfies the senses. On the contrary we end up spending our valuable time chasing after inputs which do not matter to our goals in the longer term. Therefore, whenever your senses crave for a new experience, take 2 to 3 deep breaths and ask them to relax in the present moment. You can use the mantra, "No New News" to remind yourself not to be constantly tempted. News here indicates updates.

Most of the times, people indulge in gadgets to escape from boredom, stress and unpleasant feelings. This escapism can become addictive. At such times, it is important to face our emotions as they are and feel them fully. Whenever the urge to indulge in gadgets arises, delay it for some time. Even if your senses try to overpower you, don't give in to them. This small delay will bring about a radical change. It will not only help to break this tendency but also help unleash our latent potential.

Gadgets are continuously reinforcing the belief that we are this limited body-mind. This is not the truth. The truth is that we are the limitless Self, Consciousness and being in the experience of the Self is more important than uploading our Selfie (a self portrait).

As per the epic Ramayana, Lord Rama went on a 14-years exile. Can you from time to time go on a 14-minutes mini-exile? Going on an exile does not mean going away to the jungle. It is an exile into your own mind. Going on a mini-exile is to just be in the present moment, free from gadgets. During this mini-exile of 14 minutes several times in a day, banish your gadgets. Instead, practice meditation in the marketplace, spirituality in the stock exchange, bhakti in the boardroom, tranquility in the theatre. In short, just be in the present moment and observe what nature is serving you at that moment. It can be an enriching, relaxing and blissful experience!

■ ■ ■

You can send your opinion or feedback on this book to:

Tejgyan Foundation
Pimpri Colony, P. O. Box 25, Pimpri, Pune – 411017
(Maharashtra), INDIA
Email: mail@tejgyan.com

APPENDIX

About Sirshree

Sirshree is the author of several spiritual books. His books have been translated in more than 10 languages and published by leading publishers such as Penguin and Hay House.

He is the founder of Tej Gyan Foundation, a not-for-profit organization committed to raising mass consciousness by spreading "Happy Thoughts" with branches in the United States, India, Europe and Asia-Pacific. Sirshree's retreats have transformed the lives of thousands and his teachings have inspired various social initiatives for raising global consciousness.

His works include more than 100 books and 2500 discourses. Various luminaries such as His Holiness the Dalai Lama, publishers Reid Tracy and Tami Simon and yoga master Dr. B.K.S Iyengar have released Sirshree's books and lauded his work. His book *The Magic of Awakening*, published by Penguin, was featured in the Limca Book of Records for being released on the same day in 9 languages.

TEJ GYAN... THE ROAD AHEAD

What is Tejgyan?

Tejgyan is the existential wisdom of the ultimate truth, which is beyond duality. In today's world, there are a lot of people who feel disharmony and are desperately trying to achieve some balance in an unpredictable life. Tejgyan helps them in harmonizing with their true nature, the Self, thereby restoring balance in all aspects of their life.

And then there are those who are successful but feel a sense of emptiness or void within. Tejgyan provides them fulfillment and helps them to embark on a journey towards self-realization. There are others who feel lost and are seeking the meaning of life. Tejgyan helps them to realize the true purpose of human life.

All this is possible with Tejgyan due to a very simple reason. The experience of the ultimate truth is always available. The direct experience of this truth or self-realization is possible provided the right method is known. Tejgyan is that method, that understanding. At Tej Gyan Foundation, Sirshree imparts this understanding through a System for Wisdom – a series of retreats that guides participants step by step.

Magic of Awakening Retreat

Magic of Awakening is the flagship self-realization retreat offered by Tej Gyan Foundation where participants gain access to the experience of the Self and learn to live in the present every moment. The retreat is conducted in two languages – Hindi and English. The teachings of the retreat are non-denominational (secular).

Participate in the *Magic of Awakening* retreat to attain the ageless wisdom through a unique and simple 'System for Wisdom' so that you can:

1. Live from pure and still presence allowing the natural qualities of Consciousness, viz. peace, love, joy, compassion, abundance and creativity to manifest.
2. Acquire simple tools to use in everyday life which help quieten the chattering mind, revealing your true nature.

3. Get practical techniques to gain access to pure presence at will and connect to the source of all answers (the inner guru).
4. Discover the missing links in the practices of meditation *(dhyana)*, action *(karma)*, wisdom *(gyana)* and devotion *(bhakti)*.
5. Understand the nature of your body-mind mechanism to attain freedom from tendencies and patterns.
6. Learn practical methods to shift from mind-centred living to consciousness-centred living.

This residential retreat is held for 3-5 days at the foundation's MaNaN Ashram amidst the glory of mountains and the pristine beauty of nature. This ashram is located at the outskirts of the city of Pune in India, and is well connected by air, road and rail. The retreat is also held at other centres of Tej Gyan Foundation across the world.

For retreats in English email: ma@tejgyan.com

For retreats in Hindi, contact +91 9921008060 or email mail@tejgyan.com

A Mini retreat is also conducted, especially for teens (14-17 years) during summer and winter vacations.

Register online for all the above retreats at www.tejgyan.org

MaNaN Ashram :

Survey No. 43, Sanas Nagar, Nandoshi gaon, Kirkatwadi Phata, Sinhagad Road, Tal. Haveli, Dist. Pune 411024, Maharashtra, India.
Contact No.: 992100 8060.

About Tej Gyan Foundation

Tej Gyan Foundation (TGF) was established with the mission of creating a highly evolved society through all-round self development of every individual that transforms all the facets of his/her life. It is a non-profit organization founded on the teachings of Sirshree. The foundation has received the ISO Certification (ISO 9001:2008) for its system of imparting wisdom. It has centres all across India as well as in other countries. The motto of Tej Gyan Foundation is 'Happy Thoughts'.

TGF is creating a highly evolved society through:

- Tejgyan Programs (Retreats, Courses, Television and Radio Programs, Podcasts)

- Tejgyan Products (Books, Tapes, Audio/Video CDs)

- Tejgyan Projects (Value Education, Women Empowerment, Peace Initiatives)

The foundation undertakes various projects to elevate the level of consciousness among school students, youth, women, senior citizens, teachers, doctors, leaders, organizations, police force, prisoners, etc.

♦♦♦

Books can be delivered at your doorstep by registered post or courier. You can request for the same through postal money order or pay by VPP. Please send the money order to either of the following two addresses:

WOW Publishings Pvt. Ltd.

1. Registered Office: E-4, Vaibhav Nagar, Near Tapovan Mandir, Pimpri, Pune 411017.

2. Post Box No. 36, Pimpri Colony Post Office, Pimpri, Pune 411017.

Phone No. : 9011013210 / 9623457873

YOU CAN ALSO ORDER YOUR COPY AT THE ONLINE STORE:

Log in at: www.gethappythoughts.org

*Free Shipping plus 10% Discount on purchases above Rs. 300/-.

Now you can register online for the following retreats

Maha Aasmani Niwasi Shivir
(5 Days Residential Retreat in Hindi)

Magic of Awakening Retreat
(3 Days Residential Retreat In English)

Mini Maha Aasmani Shivir
3 Days (Residential) Retreat for Teens

🔍 www.tejgyan.org

listen to profound truth by Sirshree - the author of the bestseller *The Source* on

SANSKAR TV CHANNEL
Mon to Sat 6.30 - 6.50 p.m.
Sun 8.10 - 8.30 p.m.

www.tejgyan.org
www.gethappythoughts.org

To listen to Sirshree's discourses on YouTube,
Visit: www.youtube.com/tejgyan

For further details contact:

Tejgyan Global Foundation

Registered Office:

Happy Thoughts Building, Vikrant Complex, Near Tapovan Mandir, Pimpri, Pune 411017, Maharashtra, India.
Contact No.: 020-27411240, 27412576
Email: mail@tejgyan.com

MaNaN Ashram:

Survey No. 43, Sanas Nagar, Nandoshi gaon, Kirkatwadi Phata, Sinhagad Road, Tal. Haveli, Dist. Pune 411024, Maharashtra, India.
Contact No.: 992100 8060.

Hyderabad: 9885558100, **Bangalore:** 9880412588,
Delhi: 9891059875, **Nashik:** 9326967980, **Mumbai:** 9373440985

For accessing our unique 'System for Wisdom'
from Self-help to Self-realization, please follow us on:

happy thoughts	Website	www.tejgyan.org
YouTube	Video Channel	www.youtube.com/tejgyan
facebook	Social networking	www.facebook.com/tejgyan
twitter	Social networking	www.twitter.com/sirshree
Internet Radio	Internet Radio	http://www.tejgyan.org internetradio.aspx

Online shopping
www.gethappythoughts.org

Please pray for World Peace along with thousands of others at 09:09 a.m. and p.m. every day.

www.ingramcontent.com/pod-product-compliance
Lightning Source LLC
LaVergne TN
LVHW040154080526
838202LV00042B/3153